Divided
We Fall

Alan Gibbons

Orion
Children's Books

First published in Great Britain in 1998
by Orion Children's Books
Reissued in Great Britain in 2010
by Orion Children's Books
a division of the Orion Publishing Group Ltd
Orion House
5 Upper St Martin's Lane
London WC2H 9EA
An Hachette UK company

978-1-4440-0177-8

A catalogue record for this book is available from the British Library.

www.orionbooks.co.uk

Rough Diamonds

PART ONE

Going Up

One

Some people think they've got it made. Others know they have. But if you live somewhere like the Diamond you grow up knowing you've got to make it yourself. Either that, or you sink faster than a fish in a lead waistcoat. The footy team that I play for, the Rough Diamonds, is full of kids who know that if they're going to be heard they've got to blow their own trumpet. Let's face it, nobody else is going to do it for us, are they?

Our manager, Ronnie Mintoe, doesn't like me talking like that. He's an easy-going sort and he says I've got a chip on my shoulder. You know what I say – only one? Come off it, Ron, I've got enough to keep McDonald's going for a month! What does he expect, anyway? I was just starting juniors when my dad cleared off. That's right, he just upped and went. He doesn't surface again for five years, and then it's as a bodyguard for one of our friendly neighbourhood hard men, the low-life by the name of Lee Ramage. Suddenly I'm Kev McGovern, the kid with pure evil running in his veins. I've lost track of the number of times people have said it: what do you expect with a father like that?

What's more, my dad's idea of family life is a phone call once in a blue moon. If we're lucky. As if that wasn't bad enough, this Lee Ramage character my dad works for has a kid brother, Andy, and he takes after the rest of his family. A Mutant Ninja Ratbag with knobs on. An ordinary name like Andy doesn't suit him one bit. To the rest of us he's Brain Damage, the kid from hell. Honestly, if you took all the muck and dreck the world's got and laced it with the venom of a major viper colony you'd have BD. I hate his guts – and it's mutual. We've had this vendetta going ever since I moved up to the Diamond. For a while I thought I'd managed to shut him up for good. He'd been thieving and was hiding hooky gear in Lee's lock-up. He never told Lee, either. Thanks to me, the police got interested and suddenly Brain Damage has got to keep his head down. Lee wasn't too happy with his little brother for attracting the heat.

Peace didn't break out for long, though. By mid-February the quiet times were over and Brain Damage was starting to make a nuisance of himself at school, a sure sign that Mr Malice was out of hibernation. I did have one thing to be thankful for. Andy Ramage was more Damage than Brain. He didn't have the wits to put one over on me, though a new arrival at school was about to add cunning to Brain Damage's aggro.

Anyway, that's the Diamond for you. Never a dull moment. By now you're probably thinking the place is full of crazies, a kind of psycho gulch. Not really, it's just ordinary people trying to keep their heads above water. Like my mum, for instance, and most of my mates' parents. There are two sorts of people on the Diamond, really. There's the Monster Raving Thug Party. That's the Ramages, and a few other families like them. Then there are the Normals. My cousin Cheryl, she's a Normal. So's our winger Bashir, and he manages it even though his family had to flee from some war in Africa in a place called Somalia. He doesn't talk about it much, but sometimes you just know it's left its mark on him.

As for my mate Jamie Moore, one of our strikers, I'd always thought he was the ultimate normal. In fact, I used to think the Moores invented normality. Round their house it was all athletics, swimming and footy trophies that Jamie had won, and framed snapes of holidays in Spain and Portugal. Jamie's got an older brother, Phil, but I don't see him very often. Courting, I suppose. Families like the Moores might have had to struggle for their little luxuries,

— 4 —

but they were straight. You know the sort of thing. Bought their own house. Improved it every couple of years when they had the cash. They're not like my old man. They play by different rules. No clearing off on their kids. No crooked deals. Nothing out of the ordinary.

At least, that's what I thought until events blew apart everything I'd always believed about them, and made me realise I didn't know Jamie half as well as I thought I did. The funny thing is, for all its reputation, the Diamond's got far more Normals than Thuggies. Round the north end of the city they talk about the Diamond as if it's some sort of Devil's Island, and everybody who lives there is a died-in-the-wool criminal.

I suppose I've always had a foot in both camps. Mum's a Normal, but Dad's a Thuggie and then some, and since he came back they've been fighting a civil war for my soul. For a while I'd been moving Mum's way, keeping my nose clean at school and avoiding aggro on the street. My cousin Cheryl, the original Goody-Two-Shoes Kid, she thought I was saved. Hallelujah! Then just when everything seemed to be looking up along came life to knock me back down and make me think again.

It had all been going too well, you see. Dad had actually taken me and Gareth out a couple of times. I thought for a while he was taking a real interest in us. I mean, he'd actually kept a promise! Brain Damage was stirring, but he still wasn't quite his old self, more a nettle sting than swig of arsenic. What's more, the Diamonds were really motoring. As captain, I was leading from the front. I was the Guv'nor, a workaholic midfield general in the yellow and blue of Brazil. Well, if you're going to wear somebody's colours on your back, it might as well be the best. So we adopted the kit worn by Jairzinho and Pele, Juninho and Romario. The colours seemed to be doing the trick. We were off the bottom of the league and hoping for mid-table respectability by the end of the season. Even better, we were playing some neat stuff and there was a chance we could progress in the Challenge Cup. I was secretly thinking we might have a realistic chance of winning it, but I never told anybody. I didn't want to tempt fate.

That's when the Diamonds had to face up to one of their greatest tests. It looked like costing me more than the Challenge Cup. I was about to lose one of the best friends I'd ever had, half the backbone of the side and maybe any chance of making it as a Normal.

Two

Kev threw his hands up in frustration. It wasn't the first time.

'What's with Jamie today, Guv?' asked Dave Lafferty, turning sadly back towards the centre circle after another goal-scoring opportunity had gone begging.

'You've got me,' said Kev, stamping a divot back into place. He'd cut it up with his studs in a fit of pique as Jamie fluffed his shot yet again. 'He's left his shooting boots at home, that's for sure.'

He watched the Northend United goalie retrieving the ball. The big dope couldn't believe his luck. The Diamonds were giving his defenders the run-around, but they just couldn't convert the pressure into goals. The Diamonds had had at least 70 per cent of the possession, but there was still nothing to show for it. Not a sausage. At nil–all, the Challenge Cup quarter-final hung in the balance.

'Something wrong, Jay?' asked Kev.

No answer.

'Jamie?'

Jamie gave a shake of the head, like he was coming out of a trance. 'Sorry, Guv, did you say something?'

'Just wondering if everything was all right.'

'Yes, fine. Having a bummer of a game, that's all.'

Kev nodded sympathetically. He'd had a few of them in his time. Then there was a flurry of activity ahead of him. Suddenly he wasn't thinking about Jamie any more. United had the ball ten yards inside the Diamonds' half. The lad on the ball spread the play right to left and made a run towards the penalty area. Getting on his toes, Kev tracked him.

'Cover the front men,' he bawled at the centre-backs. It wasn't a moment too soon. Gordon Jones was already coming out, tempted by the run from mid-field. He was going to leave Daz completely exposed in goal. 'It's all right, Gord, leave this one to me. I've got him.'

United chipped the ball forward, but Kev had seen the danger. He came in with a crunching challenge and shoved the ball back out to the left. One of the United forwards went for the ball, but Kev wasn't about to give up. He stuck out a leg and pushed it towards the touch-line. After that, he just had to tidy up and slot it to Jamie. Only Jamie was caught napping by the United full-back, who surged forward and whipped it in at pace. Luckily for the Diamonds.

Gord was alive to it, and nodded it out for a corner. 'What's Jamie playing at?' he demanded. 'Half asleep if you're asking me.'

'Nobody *was* asking you,' Kev snapped. Jamie might be playing like a tortoise with four wooden legs, but he was still his mate, one of the few kids who'd stood by him when he first arrived on the Diamond.

'Sorry for breathing,' said Gord.

Seeing the wounded look, Kev thought better of his

show of temper. 'It's all right, Gord. I'm in a bit of a nark with him myself. Good clearance, by the way.'

Gord smiled. That's the ticket, thought Guv. Make somebody feel good about themselves, and they'll play the better for it. The United cross came over towards the near post, but Daz Kemble was on top form in the Diamonds goal and he collected it effortlessly. He hadn't had much to do that Sunday morning, but when questions were asked he was always there with the answer. Looking up, Daz spotted their little winger Bashir out on the left flank, and distributed it long. Bashir was playing a blinder, going past the United defenders at will. The attack didn't come to anything, though. The ref's whistle saw to that. Half-time.

'I think we've been here before,' said Ronnie Mintoe. 'Loads of possession, but no goals.'

Jamie was staring at the ground. The manager's team talk clearly made uncomfortable listening.

'We'll get it sorted,' said Kev. 'We're not getting the run of the ball.'

Ronnie looked sceptical, but he wasn't arguing. 'I'll give it ten minutes,' he said. 'Then I'll be making some changes.'

It didn't take ten minutes for him to make the first substitution of the match. Jamie just couldn't get into the game. First Bash dropped a lovely cross right at his feet, but Jamie allowed it to bounce harmlessly out of play. Then Dave Lafferty rolled the ball to him in the box. It was a sitter, but once again Jamie passed it up. It was like he was on another planet, one with times-ten gravity. Or one where the human leg hadn't been invented yet.

'Right,' said Ronnie. 'I've seen enough. Come on, Jamie lad, time to give somebody else a chance.'

Normally Jamie would have been arguing all the way

to the touch-line, but he went without a murmur. Kev couldn't weigh him up at all. He couldn't put his finger on it, but he had a feeling that this had been building up for a while. It was little things really. You couldn't rely on Jamie any more. His moods went up and down like a yo-yo.

'Kevin,' said Ronnie as the substitution was being made. 'Try Joey up front. Mattie here can take his place in defence.'

Kev gave Mattie Hughes a cool stare. His defensive play was nothing to write home about, but he was better than their other sub, Carl Bain. *Anybody* was better than Carl. 'You sure about Joey in attack?' he asked. 'He isn't very tall.'

'Quick, though,' said Ronnie. 'Give it a go. We'll change things round if it doesn't work.'

'You sure you can't leave Jamie on?' asked Kev.

'Oh, I'm sure, all right,' said Ronnie. 'Besides, I've already informed the ref. Now get out there and snatch us that goal.'

Kev nodded and trotted away. As play re-started, Jamie was standing next to Ronnie with his anorak over his shoulders. He wasn't even watching the match. He was miles away. He had something on his mind all right, and it was having the weirdest effect on him. Jamie could change quicker than a werewolf just lately.

'You're in attack,' Kev told Joey.

'You what?'

'You're in attack. Ronnie says.'

Joey stared across at the manager. 'Has he gone soft in the head, or something?'

'Beats me,' said Kev. 'Anyway, he's the boss so do as you're told.'

As Joey joined Dave Lafferty up front, Kev found

Jamie's behaviour nagging away at him. It was unsettling having a werewolf for a mate.

'Some substitution,' grunted Anthony Glover, glaring at Mattie. 'That spare part for our Jamie.'

Ant was Jamie's cousin, and he took the replacement of a member of the family as a personal insult.

'Tell Ronnie, not me,' said Kev tetchily.

'Don't worry,' said Ant. 'I will.'

Meanwhile, Bashir had won a throw-in on the left. Kev jogged into space and raised his arm. Bash didn't let him down. He found Kev with the throw.

'Guv, Guv!' shouted Dave excitedly.

But Joey was better placed on the edge of the area. Kev chipped the ball over the closing defenders and ran on in expectation of a return pass. To everybody's surprise Joey shuffled his feet and hit the dropping ball first time.

The volley clipped the angle of bar and upright and cannoned back into play for one of the United centre-backs to smash it out of play.

Dave gave a low whistle. 'Some shot, Joey, I never knew you had it in you.'

Joey was staring at the goalpost.

'You know what?' said Kev. 'Neither did Joey.'

Jimmy Mintoe rubbed the ball with his sleeve and launched a long throw-in towards the penalty area. Dave found himself with his back to goal, but that didn't stop him. He flung himself into an overhead kick and connected crisply. The shot hit the United goalie in the stomach, making him drop gratefully to the ground, smothering the ball.

'Jammy beggar!' said Kev.

'Jammy nothing,' said the goalie. 'I meant that.'

'Oh yeah, and the moon's made of banana yoghurt.'

The Diamond attackers chuckled, but in the back of

everyone's mind there was a nagging thought. What if this just wasn't their day?

It was John O'Hara who finally gave voice to their anxieties. 'I don't believe this,' he groaned. 'What's it going to take for us to score?'

'A bit of positive thinking,' said Kev. 'Something we don't get off you too often.'

Prickly wasn't the word for Kev at that moment. Jamie's loss of form had set him on edge. He was like a human firework and it wouldn't take much to light the blue touch-paper.

'Now,' said Kev, clapping his hands. 'If we're going to get through to the last four in this competition we're going to have to work for it.'

Bashir *was* working. Before the kick-off one of the United players had called him a black something-or-other. It was something Bashir had had to get used to, but he wasn't *that* used to it and he was determined to ram the insult back down his antangonist's throat. He hared off down the wing with the ball at his feet then unexpectedly cut infield. It wasn't just United who were taken by surprise. So were the Diamonds. They'd got used to Bashir's line-hugging runs. Sprint, dribble and cross – that was his game. An incisive move on goal didn't seem his style at all. He was the youngest player in the Diamonds team, and probably the slightest in build. But with only the goalie to beat, that didn't seem to matter one bit.

'Hit it, Bash!' yelled Kev.

Bashir nodded and struck the ball sweetly to the keeper's right. It was in the net. He raised one hand and started walking towards the centre circle. Cool as you like.

Some of the others were less composed. 'Goalazzo!'

bawled Ratso, the Diamond's clown prince. 'And the semi-final slot belongs to the Diamonds.'

Only it didn't. Not yet. Ratso was well into his Series A commentator impression before anybody realized that the ref had blown for off-side. Bashir turned and stared in disbelief.

'Off-side!' cried Kev. 'Who?'

The ref pointed his whistle towards Joey who was standing alone on the right touch-line.

'But he was miles away. He was never interfering with play.'

'In my opinion,' said the ref huffily, 'he was clearly off-side.'

'And in my opinion,' Kev retorted, 'you're a berk.'

'Stop right there,' said the ref.

Kev was walking away. His neck was burning. He knew he'd gone too far.

'I said,' the ref insisted, 'come here.'

'What for?' cried Kev. He'd been stupid, but he wasn't about to back down. 'To get you a new pair of glasses?'

'Right, that's it,' said the ref. 'You've just earned yourself a booking.'

Kev was about to argue back but Dave Lafferty was already dragging him away.

'Behave yourself, Guv,' said Dave. 'You've already got eight disciplinary points.'

'So what?'

'So if we do get to the semis,' Dave answered, 'you could find yourself suspended. One sending off and you miss a game.'

Dave's warning did the trick. Kev might be hot-headed, but he wasn't about to jeopardize his side's chance of getting to the Challenge Cup Final.

'OK,' he said. 'I'll keep my nose clean. It was a bad decision, though.'

'Diabolical,' Dave agreed. 'But the ref isn't going to change his mind, is he?'

Kev eyed the ref, a PE teacher from Scarisbrick High and a stickler for discipline.

'Suppose not.'

The off-side decision seemed to have taken the wind out of the Diamond's sails and they found themselves on the back foot. For the first time in the match they were under sustained United pressure. Ant scrambled one shot off the line and Daz palmed another narrowly over. As the United winger placed the corner, everybody except Dave was back defending.

'Push up,' ordered Kev. 'We're getting in each other's way. Ratso, John, cover the run from the edge of the area.'

His warning came too late. The corner was played deep and the United skipper ran forward to meet it. He couldn't have struck the ball better. As it looped over the heads of the defence it was bending all the way. Definitely goal-bound. Kev could feel his knees slacken under him. They'd blown it.

But he'd reckoned without Daz.

'Mine!' he roared, propelling himself into the air and throwing out a shovel-like hand. He tipped it on to the top of the crossbar and out of play.

'Now who's jammy?' asked the United skipper. 'He had no right to get to that.'

Nobody was arguing. Kev knew it had been a let-off.

The second corner was met by Gord at the near post. His header cleared the penalty area and Joey Bannen seized on it. Looking up, he saw Dave Lafferty lurking on the half-way line with only one marker.

'Launch it, Joey,' yelled Kev.

But Joey had already released it. As Dave wheeled away from his marker, it was a chase between him and the goalie. The keeper was favourite all the way, but Dave had one thing going for him. Iron determination. He reached the ball a split-second before the goalie and flicked it over him. The ball hung for an agonizing moment, then dropped into the net.

It was one–nil. Dave's celebration was typical of him, an arrogant stroll through the United defence with his arms raised. Like Moses parting the Red Sea.

'How long to go?' Kev shouted to Ronnie.

'Two minutes,' said Ronnie. 'Just keep your concentration.'

'Don't worry,' said Kev. 'We won't let it slip now.'

They didn't. Every member of the side was up for it, harrying the United players the moment they got the ball, denying them the space to build their attacks. By the time the whistle went for full-time, United hadn't managed a decent attack.

'We've done it,' whooped Kev. 'We're through to the semi-finals.'

'You don't think …' Ratso began.

'What, win it you mean?' said Kev dismissively, 'Nah.'

But that was only for public consumption. Privately, he was beginning to think exactly that.

'Great goal, Dave,' he said. 'And a great pass, Joey.'

'Thanks,' said Joey.

'Come to think of it,' said Kev. 'We all played well. Every one of us.'

That's when he saw Jamie, alone and forgotten on the touch-line.

Well, nearly everyone.

Three

Jamie hovered on the edge of the post-match celebrations. He was on the outside looking in.

'It should have been two–nil,' Ratso was arguing. 'That run of Bashir's deserved a goal. Off-side my foot.'

Bashir smiled. He had his feet planted firmly on the ground and winning was what mattered. By any means necessary. 'We won, and that's all there is to it.'

'It would have been nice to have had a two-goal cushion,' said Jimmy Mintoe. 'Uncle Ron was having kittens the last few minutes.'

'He needn't have worried,' said Ant. 'Daz had everything covered.'

'Yes,' said Gord. 'How *did* you get to that shot near the end?'

Daz just tapped the side of his nose. 'Trade secret, Gordie, trade secret.'

'Behave,' snorted Joey Barinen. 'You just threw yourself and prayed.'

Daz gave a low chuckle. 'Some prayer, though, wasn't it?'

'It was a save and a half,' said Guv. 'We were sound. Tight and disciplined. Things are definitely coming together.'

For Jamie standing numbly in his one-boy force field, that didn't ring true. Life was more than a football match, and in his eyes things were falling apart. And fast.

'Hey, Jay,' shouted Ant. 'Fancy going up the Rec?'

The Rec was a playing field across the main road from the Diamond estate. The lads usually kicked a ball around on the grounds of South Road Community

Centre, but when they felt like a change it was the Rec.

'Dunno. Maybe. Are you going, Guv?'

'I can't,' Kev answered. 'Not this afternoon. My dad's supposed to be taking me and Gareth out. He promised us a trip to the Blue Moon Diner.'

'Think he'll show?' asked Jamie.

Kev darted a ferocious look in his direction. What was with Jamie today? 'He'll be there,' he answered frostily. 'So are you walking up?'

Jamie sighed. It was wise to keep off the subject of Kev's dad. He tapped Ant on the shoulder. 'I may just see you over the Rec, but don't hang around for me.'

'Why?' asked Ant. 'Have you got something else on?'

He hadn't, but things at home weren't good. He didn't want to make promises he might have to break. 'No, but we might be going out.'

'Funny,' said Ant. 'Uncle Billy never mentioned it.'

Ant's Uncle Billy was Jamie's dad, and he was always round at Ant's house. The Moores, brother and sister, were as close as pilchards in a can.

'Dad doesn't tell Aunty Irene everything,' said Jamie.

Ant gave him a funny look, then set off down Jacob's Lane with John O'Hara and Jimmy Mintoe. 'Suit yourself. You know where we'll be.'

Jamie accompanied Bash and Kev to the garages where they split up.

'See you, Jay,' shouted Kev.

'Yes, see you, Guv. See you, Bash.'

Jamie was almost glad to see the back of his mates. He usually loved the team banter, but that morning it had echoed dully in his brain, like somebody taunting him from far away. He remembered the way his mum talked about *those heads of hers*. Sometimes the headache got so bad she just wanted to close her eyes and go to sleep. For a very long time.

That's the way it had been for Jamie. He wanted to be out of things. Maybe forever. Everything, just everything, had been too much trouble. That went for Ratso's jokes, John's moaning, even Guv's concern. In fact it had gone for every single thing about the team. It wasn't fair, either. It wasn't the team's fault that life stank. It was his mum and dad's.

'Stupid rotten letter,' Jamie snarled out loud.

If it had only come on a weekday, there would have been none of this trouble. Dad would have been at work and Mum would have had time to hide it with her other mementoes of Phil. But it had arrived on Saturday morning. It had looked innocent enough, a brown vellum envelope addressed to Mrs J. Moore. But when Dad discovered Mum reading it, the balloon really went up.

'Stupid rotten letter,' Jamie said again. This time he accompanied his words with a savage kick against the front gate of the nearest house.

'Oi, what do you think you're playing at?' came an outraged cry.

Jamie saw the householder's face at the window. Any minute he would be out of his front door. Fed up or not, Jamie knew better than to hang about. He didn't stop running until he reached home.

'Old beggar,' he muttered, getting a belated shot at the man who'd put him to flight. 'They're all the same. Always on your back. Stupid, stupid old beggars.'

He trudged down the path and shoved open the back door. That's when he heard his dad.

'So how many of these have you had?' he was asking.

Jamie winced. He was still going on about the letter. 'How many?'

Then it was Mum's turn. 'I've told you, Bill, it's the first since he left home.'

'Expect me to believe that, do you? You must think I'm soft, woman.'

Jamie moved to the far wall. From there, he could peer through the crack in the door and see into the living room. His dad seemed to fill the room. He was pacing back and forth brandishing the letter. As for his mum, she was sitting on the arm of the settee, pale and shrunken. She was like that, always had been, a slight figure somehow at the margin of things. Jamie thought that any minute she might just fade away altogether.

'So what else is there?' Dad demanded. 'I'll find out, you know. What else are you hiding from me?'

'Nothing, love,' said Mum.

The word *love* seemed to enrage Dad all the more. 'Think I'm going to believe that, do you? I hardly know what's going on in my own house. Like the other thing.'

Jamie frowned. His dad was always dropping hints like that, as if Mum was hiding something. Something terrible.

'Please, Bill, stop it. I've never had any secrets from you.'

'Not much you haven't. What do you call this then?'

Dad tossed the letter on to the settee. 'What's that if it isn't a secret? And where's the rest of it?'

Mum's eyes widened. 'That's all there is.'

'So why's there a PTO at the bottom? Tell me that.'

Mum just stared.

'Well?'

'I don't ...'

Dad was tapping his forehead furiously. 'You're not stupid, are you, Julie? It says PTO but there's nothing on the back. So that means there must have been another page.'

'Honest to God, Billy, that's all there was.'

Jamie caught his breath. He loved his dad. He was never too busy to go fishing or run him and his mates somewhere. So how come he was so heavy with Mum all the time?

'It's just a bit of a note,' she said in that quiet way of hers. As if raising her voice would bring the roof down round her ears. 'He just wanted to write and tell me he was safe and well. You know he can't talk to you.'

'Oh, that's a good way of putting it, that is. And whose fault was it in the first place, eh? If he's no son of mine, who's to blame?'

'Billy, don't do this.'

Jamie heard his dad's voice rise to a cry of pure rage. '*Me* do it! Got it back to front, haven't you, Julie? I wasn't the one who started this.'

Suddenly Jamie couldn't stand it any longer. Dropping his bag on the kitchen floor he retreated into the back garden. He walked to the shed and slid down, squatting on the ground with his back against it. Even there he could hear the row, but only as muffled, meaningless noise, like somebody pounding on a wall. It wasn't pleasant, but he preferred it that way. At least he didn't have to listen to them tearing one another apart. He didn't have to listen to the words, the awful words that seemed to cut into his flesh. It was ten, maybe fifteen minutes before it was safe to go back inside. The green light was his dad's departure. Jamie saw him storm out of the house, slamming the back door behind him. Moments later he heard their K reg Cavalier cough into life. It was safe to go in.

'Mum, you there?'

The house was very quiet after the fury of the row. Too quiet. Panic gripped him. He didn't know where it came from, this feeling that something could go

— 19 —

horribly wrong, but it was always there, a dull, nagging anxiety.

'Mum, are you all right?'

He crossed the living room floor and shouted up the stairs.

'Mum?'

'Up here, love.'

He found her in his parents' room. She had a shoe-box on her lap and she was flicking through some old photos. The ones she'd had to take out of the album to save them from destruction.

'These the ones of Phil?' Jamie asked.

Mum nodded.

'I thought Dad had thrown them away.'

'He would have done. Don't tell him I've still got them, will you?'

Jamie hovered uncertainly beside her. 'Of course not. What do you think I am?'

That's when he noticed the sheet of paper on the bed.

'Poor love,' said Mum, fingering it. 'I wonder where he is.'

'Is that ...?'

'The second page of the letter. When your dad caught me reading it, I managed to shove this page in my pocket.'

'Anything important?'

Mum hesitated.

'I won't split on you. Honest.'

'You mustn't say a word, son, because if you did ...'

'I won't let you down, Mum.'

A thin smile told him he'd got his way.

'Just this.'

Jamie read it: *I'll phone soon. When* he's *out.* It even mentioned a couple of days.

'I bet he's still round here somewhere,' he said.

'Maybe.'

'Why, where do you think he is?'

Mum shook her head. 'I dread to think. He had nowhere to go.'

'He's got mates,' said Jamie reassuringly.

'Don't you think I've tried them,' said Mum. 'Nobody's seen him. At least they say they haven't. Not since ...'

She didn't finish. There was no need. Jamie would never forget the night his older brother Phil got thrown out. Things had started well enough. The whole family had watched the Liverpool game. They were staunch Evertonians, but they wished their rivals from across Stanley Park well as they tried to progress in the Cup-winners Cup. Jamie had gone to bed happy. A thumping victory over European opposition. Then, in what must have been the early hours of the morning he'd been woken by raised voices downstairs. In his half-awake state Jamie had thought it was thunder at first. The city had been swept by storms for the best part of a week and sheet lightning was flashing behind the curtains. Jamie had listened to the rain on the window panes. It soon became obvious it was voices he could hear. Angry ones.

'He'll be OK,' Jamie reassured his mum. 'I know he will.'

But as he looked down at her, he knew nothing of the sort. He remembered the fearful walk downstairs to see what was going on. He remembered his dad driving Phil across the room with slaps and punches. Last of all he remembered Phil turning and fleeing into the night. And the words he said as he vanished into the pouring rain and the booming wind.

'I hate you. I'll hate you forever.'

—— 21 ——

That was three weeks ago, and Jamie still didn't know why Phil had left.

'Mum, why did Phil go?'

Mum closed the shoe-box and returned it to its hiding place behind her dressing-table. 'He had a row with your dad. I told you.'

Jamie hated their rows. He had done all his life. Even when he was little he used to come up to Mum and ask her his fearful question: *You're not going to split up, are you?*

'But what was it about?' he asked.

'You know they never got on.'

Jamie ground his teeth. He'd been down this avenue before. There was so much more to Phil's departure, but nobody was talking.

'Why, though?'

Mum stood up abruptly and made for the door. 'I've got to get the dinner on.'

'What's going on, Mum? Why won't you talk?'

She glanced back at him, then continued downstairs. Conversation over.

'Stupid!' he announced to the four walls.

It really did seem that the whole world was stupid.

Four

Dad didn't show.

Me and Gareth were sitting there like complete lemons. We must have waited for over an hour before we finally gave up on him. Gareth wasn't that bothered. He was only a baby when Dad cleared off, so he's had to grow up without him. I sometimes wish I had. It'd be good not to care. Easier. I tell you, it really cuts me up living like this. If he was going to walk back into our lives, why couldn't he do it properly? All these years waiting and it was a hero I wanted. Not Lee Ramage's lackey.

Cheryl was round with Aunty Pat. Dead sympathetic, of course, but that only made it worse. I know exactly what they think of my dad. Not much. And when you're a loser, you don't want witnesses there.

'I'll give your dad a piece of my mind when I see him,' said Mum.

The show of anger was for my benefit. She isn't really angry. She must have got past angry years ago. No, she's just weary. It must get you like that, years of being let down.

'Forget it,' I said, picking up my football. 'I have.'

It wasn't true, of course. I was choked. I really hated him the way he did his vanishing trick on us all the time. I could feel my eyes stinging, so I had to get out before I made a fool of myself.

'You all right?' asked Cheryl, catching me at the door.

'Never better,' I told her.

'You're not upset about your dad, are you?'

'Of course not.'

'Because he isn't worth it. Your mum's the one who matters.'

'Sure. I know that.'

'Do you need some company?' she asked.

'Nah, I'm going to Jamie's.'

'Oh,' said Cheryl.

I headed for Jamie's. At the top of the Avenue I looked back at our house. I had to face it, Cheryl was right – Mum really is the only parent I've got. Only there's always this voice somewhere inside me that won't let me give up on my dad. No matter how often he breaks my heart. Mum's *the only family I've got, everybody says so. I don't need Aunty Pat or Cheryl to tell me she's the rock everything is built on. I mean, I know it already. Ever since my dad left, she's kept us going.*

But you know the trouble with rocks? Sure, they're solid and dependable. But exciting? No way. And I need exciting. I've always flown near the flame. If you don't take risks, you're nothing. I don't want to be a nothing, another divvy kid sitting in class with their hands up trying to get noticed. I want to be like I am on the football field. I never play safe. I'm always right on the edge. That's why Davie Lafferty had to warn me about getting sent off in the Northend game. There's only a half inch of space between determination and dirty play and I live in it. I want to be the Guv'nor, the one who makes things happen. What's so wrong with that? Think about it. If you met a Wizard or something and they could give you the choice between two lives, which one would you choose? The one that's like a top of the range BMW, or the rusty Lada. I know which I'd have. And that's the problem. For every moment I think of my dad as trouble, a dead-beat who can hardly remember our names, there are all the other times when I see the hero in him.

Then my head is full of pictures of his boxing medals and the cuttings out of the Echo, *and the stories about his fights with the other hard men on the estate, and the funny, mysterious way he says he's got* business *to sort out. Then there's no contest. I know men who look at life the same way Mum does. The Normals. They go to work, keep their noses clean, put their families first. My Uncle Dave for one. Or Jamie's dad. Sometimes I get so jealous of Cheryl and Jamie and their safe, reliable fathers. I'd give my right arm to have a dad like that. Then I sort of know I'll never be like that when I grow up. It does my head in really.*

Five

'I see Ronnie's been reading the FA manual again,' sighed John O'Hara.

Everybody was looking expectantly at Ronnie, waiting for his words of wisdom.

'I bet Ratso even knows which page,' said Daz.

Ratso was more an encyclopaedia of soccer than an eleven-year-old boy. 'Thirty-six,' he said. 'Forward runs – with and without the ball.'

'You're kidding, right?' said Kev.

Ratso gave the captain a level stare. He wasn't.

'Hey, Ron,' shouted Kev. 'We know where you got the training routine from. You're rumbled.'

'I don't care if you do know,' said Ronnie. 'I'm no football coach. Listen to what the experts have to say, that's my motto.'

Kev turned, smiling. That's when he saw the look on Jamie's face. Somehow Kev barely knew his moods any more. For this particular werewolf, there was a full moon every night. Whatever Jamie had twisting in his guts, it wasn't getting any better. Kev was worried about him.

'Joining our group?' he asked.

'Yes, whatever,' said Jamie.

'What's with our Jay?' whispered Ant. 'He sounds dead down.'

'I thought you might know,' said Kev.

'Not a clue,' said Ant. 'Uncle Billy was round ours last night. He never said anything.'

Kev screwed his eyes against the setting sun. 'I just wish he'd snap out of it. He's driving me nutso.'

'Me too,' said Dave Lafferty. 'I was carrying him for most of the game against Northend.'

Kev watched Jamie walking across the training-ground. It was a twilit February afternoon and most of the Diamonds were beating their chests with their arms to keep warm. Jamie wasn't even doing that. He just hung around at the edge of the session nursing his own private thoughts.

'Come on, Ron,' shouted Kev. 'Let's get on with it. I'm getting frostbite here. Bits of me are going to start dropping off in a minute.'

'Let's hope one of them is your tongue,' said Ronnie mischievously.

He quickly had them practising diagonal runs to make space. Kev watched Jamie going through his paces with all the enthusiasm of a dead rat. It wasn't lost on Ronnie, either.

'Is that it, Jamie lad?' he asked. 'That all you can manage?'

'What?'

'You look like you can't be bothered to me,' said Ron. 'Do you want to make the side this Sunday, or what?'

'Sorry,' said Jamie.

It was a thin, whining sort of apology. The sort that tells you nothing's going to change.

Ronnie wandered towards the second practice group, shaking his head. Kev recognized the gesture. He was making a mental note; Jamie was out of the reckoning.

'What's with you just lately?' Kev asked Jamie.

'I don't know what you mean.'

'Mooning round like your dog got run over, or something.'

'We haven't got a dog.'

'All right, your cat.'

'We haven't—'

Kev lost his temper. 'All right, your rotten goldfish then. All I'm saying is, you're not pulling your weight.'

Jamie shrugged his shoulders.

Kev gave up. 'You talk some sense into him, Ant.'

Ant gave Kev a sideways look. 'Me? You're joking, aren't you, Guv? He takes no notice of me, I'm only his cousin.'

'Just leave me alone, eh?' said Jamie.

And that was that. The training session carried on more or less without him. He made a few passes, but that was about the limit of his contribution. Dave looked on in despair. It wasn't what he expected from his regular strike partner.

'Jamie's been acting weird for ages,' he observed.

'Tell me about it,' said Kev. 'I can't weight him up at all.'

Ronnie finally called the boys together. 'Right lads, that'll do for now. We're losing the light, anyway.'

Kev watched the darkness closing round them, relieved only by the floodlights on the railway sidings. A group of shadowy figures caught his eye. He frowned for a moment, his instinct for trouble alerted. But he dismissed the thought immediately and turned his attention to Ronnie's talk.

'Only one change from the side that played Northend,' said Ronnie. 'I'm keeping the side that finished the game. Mattie in defence ...'

Mattie grinned. It was his first recall to the side since Gordon Jones had taken his place. '... Joey partnering Dave up front, and Jamie on the sub's bench. And if anyone is feeling hard done by ...' He glanced at Jamie. '... There's only one argument I'm about to listen to. Play yourself back into the side. OK, see you Sunday morning bright and early. Should be a good run-out for us. Red House Rovers.'

Red House were down in bottom place. The Diamonds had overtaken them and expected to give them a good hiding.

'We're looking forward to it,' said Kev. 'Aren't we, lads?' He looked around, registering the nods of agreement. Only Jamie cast a shadow over things.

'Glad to hear it,' said Ronnie. 'We'll show them what we're made of.'

Kev was half-way down South Road when he turned to Jamie. 'Are you going to tell me what's going on, or what?'

Bashir was with them, but he looked straight ahead. Bashir didn't get involved in disputes between the other boys. He was a newcomer to the estate, still feeling his way.

'I told you,' Jamie said impatiently. 'Nothing's going on. I'm going through a bad patch, that's all. I can't seem to get my game together.'

'It's your head you need to get together,' snorted Kev. Then, in an instant, his voice changed. 'Oh wonderful, that's all I need.'

Bashir had spotted the danger at the same time as Kev. 'Brain Damage.'

'Well well,' said Brain Damage. 'If it isn't my old mate the Guv'nor.'

Kev clocked the opposition. Brain Damage, Tez Cronin and a couple of their mates. Then he did a double-take. It couldn't be.

'Long time no see, McGovern.'

It was him all right.

'Costello.'

'Aw, how sweet,' came Costello's sly, needling voice. 'You remember me.'

How could Kev forget? He'd grown up on the same estate as Luke Costello, so Costello knew all about

Kev's past. The way his dad had cleared off. The way the pain of desertion had sent him off the rails. The way he'd started setting fires to get back against a stinking world that seemed determined to tread all over him. Worst of all, the way an old guy had died because of it. Kev had never meant it. It was a heart attack. The whole thing had been a horrible accident, a prank that had gone wrong, but that didn't seem to matter. Everyone blamed Kev.

'What are you doing round here?' demanded Kev.

'Haven't you heard?' asked Costello. 'I moved up here last week.'

Kev's heart squirmed in his throat. Costello, on the Diamond. it couldn't be true. They'd bumped into each other on the football field and that had been an encounter too many.

'So,' Costello continued, smiling coldly. 'We can resume our acquaintance.'

Resume our acquaintance, that was Costello all over. He wasn't soft and that's what made him dangerous, a lot more dangerous than a common or garden animal like Brain Damage.

'Get lost,' Kev told him. 'You're not living round here. I would have heard.'

'Oh, it's no wind-up,' said Costello. 'I'm here to stay. Aren't I, Andy?'

Brain Damage smirked. Kev's senses reeled at the thought of it. His two worst enemies united against him, and they hadn't taken long to get together either.

'Get out of my way,' ordered Kev.

Costello and Brain Damage stepped aside, inviting Kev, Jamie and Bashir to pass. To Kev's surprise, nothing happened. Not to him, anyway. But just as Bashir was following his friends through the gauntlet,

Tez caught his ankle. Bashir tripped and fell full length on the pacement.

'Oh sorry,' said Tez. 'I didn't see you there. You must have got lost in the dark.'

Bashir was on his feet right away, stung by the jibe. 'You did that on purpose.'

'As if I would.'

Costello chuckled.

'You know what,' said Kev, snatching his sleeve. 'We're going to settle this, right here, right now. For keeps.'

'Fine by me,' said Costello. 'Think you, Jamie and Gooly can take us, do you?'

Kev wasn't sure. Brain Damage was already at Costello's side, squaring up for a ruck. The odds weren't good, but there was no backing down. Pride saw to that. 'Think it?' snarled Kev. 'I know it.' He switched his attention from Costello to Brain Damage. 'Didn't you learn your lesson last time?'

Brain Damage didn't like to be reminded of previous defeats. 'Oh, I learnt my lesson, all right. That's the last time you get one over on me. Ever.' He leant into Kev's face. 'You landed me in our Lee's bad books with that little game of yours. Now it's pay-back time. There's a score to settle, McGovern.'

Kev still didn't like the balance of forces. He decided to back off a bit, to try to face down the opposition. No sense bringing things to a head when you haven't got the manpower. But he'd reckoned without Jamie.

'Clear off, Brain Damage,' yelled Jamie, shoving the taller boy in the chest.

Kev was taken by surprise, so much so that he almost missed the punch Costello aimed at his head. Kev leant away. He felt the air brush his face as the blow missed. Costello wasn't the street-fighter Brain

Damage was. But he had something else, a sort of sly cunning that wounded more than fists ever could.

'Call them off,' Kev panted.

'Forget it, McGovern,' said Costello. 'There's a new kid on the block.'

Again it was Jamie who upped the anti. With a shriek of rage he launched another attack, this time at Costello. He caught him with a jab. He actually drew blood. Kev saw Costello's eyes narrow. He knew that look. Now the vendetta was against both of them.

'You're going to regret that,' Costello hissed at Jamie. His threat started the fight in earnest.

Kev realized very quickly it was going against them. The addition of Costello to Brain Damage's gang had swung things in their favour.

'Now we're going to see who's boss,' Costello gloated.

It didn't happen. Kev was aware of a car pulling up, then a man's voice.

'What's going on here?'

It was Ronnie. 'Who's there? Kevin, Bashir, that you?'

Costello watched Ronnie approaching. 'Seventh Cavalry, eh? I'll catch you again, McGovern. You *and* Mr Angry here.' He meant Jamie. 'This isn't over.'

'You boys all right?' asked Ronnie.

'Yes, fine,' said Kev. 'We could have handled it. Right, lads?'

Bashir was breathing heavily and Jamie had a red mark on his cheek. They didn't look ready to handle anything. Jamie seemed to have recovered from the fit of rage that had started the fight. Regret was written all over his face.

Then, from a distance, Costello shouted: 'Hear me, McGovern, this isn't over.'

With Costello, it never was. It was six months since Kev had moved from the old estate, but their vendetta was as keen and raw as ever. It could only get worse. Especially when Costello had an animal like Brain Damage to help him.

Six

Sometimes I think I'm losing it. What was I saying about not wanting to be a Normal? I must have been off my rotten trolley. There's nothing I'd like better. Look at Jamie. He's got the lot. A mum and dad who think the sun shines out of him, holidays abroad, Christmas pressies by the truckload. And no coppers sniffing round, wondering what your dad's been up to. And that's not all. In Phil he's got a brother who cares. I wonder if I'll ever be that good to our Gareth. Makes you wonder why Jamie's acting so oddly. I mean, I'd never have expected him to act the way he did yesterday, throwing himself at Brain Damage and Costello like that. It's the werewolf again. Anyway, he's normal most of the time and I envy him for it.

OK, so some of that is down to the way my old man treats me. He phoned, you see. 'I had business.' he said.

And that was it. Business. I can guess what sort, sorting some poor divvy who owes money to Lee Ramage. Me and my big, exciting world! That's not what my dad's offering me. All he gives us is a load of grief and let-downs. And it's me and our Gareth who get dumped on. Lee stinking Ramage, he always comes first. Just because he's got a roll of the folding stuff in his back pocket.

Talking of the Ramages, Brain Damage is coming out of his shell good style − thanks to Costello. He started in Brain Damage's class on Friday. We could hear the trouble from our classroom even though his is across the corridor. They've got a student teacher in, Miss Davis, and Costello and Brain Damage were giving her a dog's life. Anyway, she threw Brain Damage out for disrupting her lesson. Not Costello, of course. He's too crafty to get caught. He just gets other people to do his dirty work. Chucking Brain Damage out didn't do much good.

There's a hole in the skirting board, so he's down on the floor calling 'Coo-ee' through it. Well, Costello's stirring things up in the classroom as well and all the kids are laughing fit to burst. Miss Davis is wondering what's setting them off. When it gets so she can't hear herself think she starts yelling for quiet. I mean, it was a complete disaster. We're talking Krakatoa, east of Bootle. In the end it got so bad Jacko, our teacher, goes to sort things out. Only Brain Damage is completely out of control by then and he tells Jacko where to get off, swears at him. As you can imagine, Jacko goes ape and sends Brain Damage to the Head. But Brain Damage doesn't fancy that either, so he runs out of school. Everybody's wondering what's going to happen on Monday.

Did I say I wanted to walk on the wild side? Seeing Costello and Brain Damage in action, I don't think so really. Give me Jamie's life any day, even if the miserable beggar doesn't know how lucky he is. Normal will do me just fine.

Seven

Jamie caught up with Kev and Bashir at the top of Owen Avenue, just before they turned towards the garages.

'I wouldn't go that way,' he told them. 'I spotted

Brain Damage. He's up to no good. There's no point inviting trouble.'

Kev smiled. This was more like the old Jamie. 'Was Costello with him?' he asked.

Jamie nodded.

'Setting up an ambush, are they?' mused Kev. 'We'll soon sort them out.'

'Behave,' said Jamie. 'There's half a dozen of the creeps. Tez and the usual crew. Oh, and this big fat mate of Costello's.'

'Jelly Wobble?'

'Yes, that's him. The one that played against us for Blessed Hearts.'

It had been a real grudge match earlier in the season, and another reason for Costello's vendetta against Kev.

'You don't really want to fight with them, do you?' Bashir asked. 'It's only twenty minutes until the kick-off.'

Kev grinned. 'Seeing as we're short of time, I think we'll live to fight another day. We'll give them the slip round the back of the Parade.'

Bashir breathed a sigh of relief. His family had had its fair share of trouble with the Ramages when they first moved in. Rubbish thrown in their garden and through the letter-box. Damage to the car. Turned-over dustbins. *Go Home* slogans painted on the gate. That sort of thing. His mum was having to get tablets off the doctor. She couldn't stand any more, and Bashir didn't want to be the one to give Brain Damage an excuse to start any aggravation up again.

The detour round South Parade prevented a fight, but not an exchange of insults. Brain Damage must have realized they weren't coming and had reached the bottom of the Parade as they turned the corner at the top. 'Done a runner, have you, McGovern? Well, you can run but you can't hide. I'll have you, lad. You *and* your divvy mates.'

'In your dreams,' Kev retorted. 'You aren't even in my league, Brain Damage.'

'He will be though,' said Costello. 'With a little help from his friends.'

Kev eyed Costello and Jelly Wobble warily. Their presence made him uneasy, but he did his best not to let it show. 'Yeah yeah,' he answered. 'I'm shaking in my boots. Listen, that's my knees you can hear knocking.' Then he gave a loud guffaw and led the way to Jacob's Lane sports ground.

All the way down the road Jamie was looking back anxiously.

'Forget them,' said Kev. 'I have.'

'Can I ask you something?' asked Jamie.

'What's that?'

'Are you as brave as you sound, or is it all an act?'

Kev sucked his teeth, then gave Jamie a sly wink. 'You'll have to figure that out for yourself, Jay. Just like Costello.'

Jamie eyed his friend. He could be really annoying sometimes.

'Feeling any better?' asked Kev.

Jamie shrugged his shoulders. Better? He wasn't prepared to go that far. He didn't really know how he felt. Mum and Dad seemed to have patched things up, and that was something of an improvement but he wasn't about to make a song and dance about it. All quiet on the Home Front. Jamie knew he was walking on thin ice, but at least the ice was holding. For now.

'Cutting it fine, aren't you?' asked an anxious Dave Lafferty, as they entered the changing-rooms.

'Just a bit of business to sort out,' said Kev brightly.

Jamie shook his head. He wished he had half of

Guv's cockiness, but he wasn't proud of his flare-up against Costello. He had enough bother at home without adding to it.

'The only business that matters is out there,' said Dave pointing towards the pitches.

Ratso had his ghetto blaster belting out a rap anthem at full volume. The pre-match rituals were in full swing.

'Ready boys?' asked Ronnie, poking his head round the door.

'Ready as we'll ever be,' said Kev. 'Come on, lads, let's roast these bozos.'

As Jamie took his place on the touch-line with the other sub, Carl Bain, he was regretting the way Mum and Dad's bust-up had affected his form. He would have given his eye teeth to be out there against Red House. They were the licking boys of the entire league. It was the ideal opportunity for an out-of-form striker to get back on track.

'Missing the action?' asked Ronnie.

Jamie didn't hear. Too preoccupied with things at home. 'What was that?'

'I asked how you felt, sitting on the sidelines.'

'Lousy.' But that wasn't just down to being dropped.

'Then you know what you've got to do. Show me you've still got it.'

'How do I do that sitting here?' asked Jamie.

'Don't worry, son,' said Ronnie. 'You'll get your chance.'

As Dave Lafferty got the game underway, Jamie remembered Kev's call to arms: *roast these bozos*. Unfortunately for the Diamonds, the bozos didn't feel like getting roasted. They took the game to the Diamonds right from the off.

Dispossessing an uncomfortable-looking Joey Bannen, they went for the jugular. Only a brave dive at the feet of the Red House striker by Daz Kemble stopped the Diamonds going one down in the first minute. Jamie glanced at Ronnie, but the manager had his eyes trained on the play.

'What was that?' demanded Kev angrily. 'Haven't you woken up yet, or something? Play up lads. Press them.'

Kev was mid-way inside his own half, trying to work the ball out of defence.

'Square ball,' shouted Jimmy Mintoe.

Kev nodded and stroked the ball out to the left. But Jimmy had taken his eye off the ball, and stumbled on it in his haste to get forward. Seizing on his error, Red House swept forward. A neat exchange of passes and they were in striking distance of goal. Looking up, the Red House winger flicked the ball into the path of an oncoming team-mate. A solidly-struck shot and the Diamonds were one–nil down.

Kev's frustration boiled over and he went after Jimmy. 'That was down to you,' he yelled, shoving Jimmy in the back. It was only when Kev noticed Dave shaking his head that he remembered his warning in the Northend game. Get into trouble and he would be facing a suspension. Apology time, he decided. 'Sorry Jim,' he said. 'I was out of order.'

Typical, thought Jamie, watching the Guv'nor's antics. Last week life was rotten and I lost my place. Now that things have calmed down and I could make a real contribution, I can't even get on the pitch.

Ronnie didn't look one bit bothered what Jamie thought. He was too busy yelling instructions.

'Get your passing together. Bring Bash into the game.'

Kev struck a long ball over the top to Dave Lafferty, the target man. Dave nodded it down neatly to Joey Bannen's feet. Joey did his bit, taking the ball in his stride and making ground towards the penalty area. Spotting Bashir out on the left, Joey spread the play.

'Good move,' said Jamie admiringly.

Bashir lofted a teasing cross into the box.

It was the sort of chance Dave wasn't about to pass up. With a glancing header he put the Diamonds on level terms. One–all.

'Better,' said Kev. 'Much better.'

Five minutes later it got better still. This time one of the Red House defenders failed to clear his lines. Dave was on him in an instant. Surging forward he went round the goalkeeper and hit it just inside the left upright. Two–one.

Suddenly the Diamonds were playing exhibition stuff, knocking it round arrogantly and letting Red House run for it.

'Sweet passing,' observed Jamie. He was dying to get on the pitch.

'Too sweet,' said Ronnie. 'Pretty to watch but it's going nowhere.' Raising his voice he shouted a warning. 'Not too fancy. Be more direct. Get it into their half.'

It came too late. Ant executed one neat flick too many and sold John O'Hara short. For the second time Red House took advantage of the error. One of their mid-fielders hit a stunning volley. Two–all.

Ronnie turned away in disgust.

'Don't worry,' said Jamie. 'We'll turn it round.'

'Fancy your chances?' asked Ronnie.

'Does a bull have horns?'

'And you're in the mood?'

Jamie thought of home and the way Dad seemed to

have decided to lower the temperature. 'What do you think?'

'Right, I'll give them ten minutes to turn things round then you're on.'

The Diamonds had a couple of chances to go ahead, but each time Red House managed to hack it clear. The pressure was all from the Diamonds but nothing was coming of it. The Lafferty-Bannen partnership wasn't working, and Joey was fading badly.

'So do I get a chance, Ron?' asked Jamie after the break-down of yet another attack.

'You're on,' said Ronnie. He strode forward. 'Kevin, tell Mattie he's off. Put Joey back in defence. I'm going to play Jamie up front.'

Kev grinned broadly, as if to say *About Time*.

'All right, Jamie,' said Ronnie, 'You've got your chance. Don't waste it.'

Jamie started his contribution to the game the moment he ran on to the pitch. He intercepted a poor clearance by the Red House keeper and his volleyed return shot grazed the outside of the post.

'Hard luck, Jay,' said Kev encouragingly. 'That was quick thinking.'

Two minutes later Jamie did more than hit the woodwork. Bashir held up the ball then threaded it into John O'Hara's path. John touched it off towards Jamie who hit it first time between the goalie's hands and the upright. Three–two.

'Sweet,' said Kev. 'Push up, lads, we've got them rocking.'

Just before half-time the Diamonds went further ahead. Kev picked out Jimmy Mintoe with a pin-point pass and ran on for the return ball. Shrugging off a defender's challenge he pushed into the penalty area and finished the move himself. Four–two.

Suddenly it was Ole football. The Diamonds were turning on the style. Bashir and Jamie in particular were giving Red House the run-around.

Jamie made it five–two, heading home a Bashir cross. Within a minute it was six–two as Jamie returned the favour, setting up Bashir for a well-deserved goal. The heads of the Red House players were drooping. Their promising start was now a distant memory. Only the half-time whistle saved them from further humiliation.

'Good enough for you, Ronnie?' asked Kev.

'Not bad,' said Ronnie, unable to conceal a smile of satisfaction.

'Not bad?' retorted Ant. 'We were excellent.'

'Don't rest on your laurels,' said Ronnie. 'Turn it on in the second half and you can improve our goal difference.'

'And boy does it need improving,' said Ratso. 'Minus twenty-six at the start of this game.'

'OK, that's the target then,' said Ronnie, doing his mental arithmetic. 'See if you can beat this shower twenty-eight–two.

Ronnie was joking, but only just. What's more, the Diamonds took him at his word. In the second half, John got in on the act with two well-taken efforts.

'Look at O'Hara,' said Jamie. 'Even old misery guts looks happy.'

When Ant made it nine–two with a near-post header from Bashir's corner, the Diamonds were walking on air. Even then it wasn't over.

'My ball,' yelled Dave Lafferty, as Jamie broke away from his marker on the edge of the penalty area.

Jamie released the ball and watched Dave collect his hat-trick. Ten–two.

Kev made it eleven with a back heel ninety seconds later, and with two minutes to go Daz left his goal for his party piece, the attacking keeper. He went up for the next corner and chested the ball into the net.

'Twelve–two,' cried Ratso. 'Twelve flipping two. The perfect performance.'

'Not quite,' said Kev. 'Jamie hasn't got his hat-trick.'

With the ref glancing at his watch, the chance came. Dave Lafferty nutmegged his marker and surged forward. He was about to stroke the ball home when the goalie brought him down. Penalty.

'And what do you think you're doing?' demanded Kev as Dave placed the ball on the spot.

'Taking the penalty,' Dave answered.

'Not this time you're not,' said Kev. 'Jamie's on his hat-trick, remember. You've got yours.'

Dave backed away reluctantly from the ball. 'Go on then, Jay. It's all yours.'

Jamie took a deep breath, jogged forward and side-footed the ball to the keeper's right.

Thirteen–two.

'Genius!' roared Ratso as the final whistle blew. 'We're the best. Simply the best.'

Kev threw his arms round Ratso and Jamie's shoulders. 'I told you we were good. Didn't I, eh? Go on, even when we were at the foot of the table, didn't I tell you we'd come out on top? We're on our way up, boys.'

For Jamie that was doubly true. A couple of days before he could have lain down and died. And that was before Costello added to his problems. Now he was walking with a swagger. He just hoped it would last.

Eight

Jamie's joy lasted as far as the front door. That's where he met his dad on the way out. It didn't take a university degree to know that something had happened.

'Anything wrong, Dad?'

'Ask your mother,' was the abrupt reply.

Jamie watched his dad climb into the driver's seat and accelerate down the street, the car rocking on its suspension. When the old man drove like that, it meant there had been a row. *Ask your mother*, that was Dad's stock answer. Jamie crossed the front doorstep.

'Oh, hello son,' said Mum as Jamie walked in.

She was reaching up to the wall unit. Jamie had a feeling she was hiding something.

'What was it this time?' asked Jamie. His voice was hard. He was fed up. The Diamonds had just won a cracking victory and he wanted to savour it. But his parents had put paid to that. Now all he could taste was ashes.

'Oh, you know, something and nothing.'

Jamie shook his head. 'You never tell me anything.' He spat the words at her. Even as he did so, he wondered what made him so angry with her. Dad was every bit as bad, but it was Mum everybody vented their anger on. Maybe it was just because she was always there. You can't take it out on somebody who's just driven off like Damon Hill.

'I'd better tidy up,' said Mum.

That was her answer to everything.

'Mind if I put the telly on?' asked Jamie. He'd decided he wasn't going to get any more sense out of her than he had off his dad.

— 42 —

'No, I'm going to vacuum upstairs.'

Jamie looked around for the remote control.

'Have you seen the clicker?' he asked.

Mum's face changed.

'What's the matter?'

'It's broken.'

'Where is it? Maybe I can fix it. It might only need new batteries.'

Mum reached on to the shelf of the wall unit. 'I think it needs more than batteries, Jamie.'

The crushed shards of black plastic in her hand were unrecognizable as the remote control.

'What happened to it?'

'It broke.'

'I know that,' said Jamie. 'How?'

Mum took a deep breath. 'Your dad stamped on it.'

'He what?'

'He stamped on it. In a fit of anger.'

Jamie stared incredulously at the remote. 'What for?'

Mum permitted herself a rare show of annoyance. 'He doesn't need a reason. Just that uncontrollable temper of his.'

Jamie wasn't having that. 'He must have done it for *something*.'

'OK,' said Mum, 'If you really must know, I think he wished it was me.'

Jamie instantly wanted to retreat. This was forbidden territory, and he wanted it to stay that way. There are some things you just don't want to know.

'What do you think of that, then?' she continued. 'He just kept stamping on it, driving his heel into it, and all the time he wanted it to be me.'

Jamie wanted her to stop. 'Don't say that, Mum.'

'Why not? It's true.'

Suddenly he was close to panic. They're funny

things, parents' lives. Sometimes they're like a foreign country, full of mysterious riches. But there are dark spaces, too, shadowy and full of menace. Jamie felt he was being dragged towards a brutal knowledge he was afraid of.

'Do you want me to tell you about your wonderful father? Do you want to know what he's really like?'

Jamie took a step back. 'Stop it, Mum. You're scaring me.'

But before she could say another word, they were both halted in their tracks by the sound of a door slamming. Dad was back.

'Don't tell him what I said,' she whispered.

Jamie could hear his dad's footsteps on the path.

'You didn't really say *anything*,' he told her.

But there had been real fear in her voice. Jamie had heard it before. Now he was beginning to wonder what put it there. The front door creaked and Mum gave Jamie a last, pleading look.

What's making you so scared, he thought.

Dad walked into the room.

What?

Nine

Well, well, so the Normals argue too, and by the look on Jamie's face this morning they do it with style. When he rolled into school he was down in the dumps again. And he'd been over the moon after the Red House game. I ask you, the kid has more ups and downs than a roller coaster. He wasn't about to give much away, but it was obviously parent trouble. Let's face it, I recognize the signs. Hissing their names through gritted teeth, that's always a dead giveaway.

I was surprised. Jamie's mum is really nice, and his dad seems a great bloke. He and Jamie go to Everton home games together, and they go fishing twice a week. So what's Jamie got to gripe about? He should try trading places with me for a few days, then he'd really have something to whinge about. I found out what Dad's business was, the big deal that mattered so much he couldn't take me and Gareth out last Sunday. Brain Damage was boasting about it. Oh, that's right, Brain Damage is still in school. A warning from the Head, and he's back in class. Mouthy with it, boasting about how his Lee sorted out some bad lads. According to him, a couple of fellers from Bootle had moved in on big brother's patch. I didn't ask what Brain Damage meant by 'patch', but I've got a pretty good idea what it's about, and it's all about as legit as the Mafia. Anyway, Lee and my dad sorted the opposition. They had to dole out a broken jaw and a couple of cracked ribs, but it looks like these Bootle lads know the score. They won't be back in a hurry.

The win over Red House seems a long time ago, for me and Jamie both. Talk about one step forward, two steps back!

Ten

Jamie knew who it was the moment the car drew up. Funny how you get to recognize the sound of your own motor.

'Hi, Dad.'

'Jump in, son.'

Jamie nodded and slid into the front passenger seat.

He threw his Everton holdall on to the back seat. As he belted up he noticed the time on the dashboard clock. 'Did you finish early, or something?'

'I've been on a training course. Some new machinery from Germany. So what have you been up to?'

'Swimming. I went straight from school with the lads.'

'Our Anthony wouldn't be one of them by any chance?'

'Yes, it was me, Ant, Guv and Bashir. Why?'

'Oh, nothing much. Just that he's going to get his eye wiped when he gets home. I've just been round your Aunty Irene's. He never told her he was going to be late back. She was going hairless. Thought he'd run under a bus or something. He's dead thoughtless, that kid.'

Jamie smiled. That's Ant. It would never occur to him to tell his mum anything.

'Fancy going to Wright's Pool this Saturday?' Dad asked, taking a right turn. 'You can invite Kevin as well if you want.'

'Yes, great, I'll ask him tomorrow.'

'Does he have his own fishing tackle?'

'No, he borrows mine.'

'Then he can have your old rod.'

'It's all right. I'll use that,' said Jamie. 'I'll lend Guv my new one.'

'You won't, you know. That was your birthday present.'

'Oh, OK.'

Jamie glanced across at his dad. He was nearly bald, but it didn't make him look old. He was thin and wiry, with sucked-in cheeks and a high forehead. Hard-looking, but in a different way to Guv's dad. Hard as in confident and self-sufficient, proud, his own man. Jamie had no worries about his dad turning out like

Tony McGovern. Straight as a die, his old man. And great to be with. At least, if you were in his good books. So what was the trouble with Phil? And Mum? Jamie frowned. For as long as he could remember, in so many different ways, he'd been asking that question. He'd been a witness to the rows, but only that. It was Mum and Phil who took the brunt of Dad's rages – never him.

Jamie knew he was his dad's favourite. That wasn't difficult, mind. Phil got it in the neck for everything. He couldn't breathe without being pounced upon. Dad had always had a downer on him. And just let Mum stick up for their oldest son! That was sure to start a row. Not that being the blue-eyed boy made Jamie feel any better. It was like there was this big hole in his family's life and it drew him to its empty depths. He had tried to pretend it didn't exist. He'd told himself it was all happy families, but the truth couldn't be buried that easily. He was walking unsteadily at its edge, scared that at any moment he might fall in and spin there forever, forced to face the secret that seemed to divide his parents.

'So we're set for Saturday?' Dad asked.

'Sorry? Oh yes, it'll be great.'

They pulled up outside the house. Jamie saw Mum twitching back the blinds and he felt a pang. The emptiness of the house was calling him, and dangling at its heart was the secret, the reason Dad had driven Phil away. Some things you just don't want to know, Jamie thought. Then, uneasily, he wondered if Phil had the strength to stay away.

'I'm having a shower.'

'Did your dad say why he's home so early?' Mum

asked Jamie. Her eyes darted nervously upstairs after him.

'Why, does it matter?'

'No, not really.'

Mum was on edge. She was trembling like a rabbit. Jamie watched her pacing the kitchen floor. Her behaviour was setting him on edge. She was acting so strangely. After a while she stopped and stared up at the ceiling, as if she could see through into the bathroom.

'I wonder what he's up to?'

That's when the phone rang. Mum fairly flew out of the kitchen. Jamie stood at the door and watched her snatch the phone.

'Hello ... hello ...' Then a catch in her voice. 'Phil ... *Phillip* ...'

Jamie watched the changing expressions on his mum's face, then the way her shoulders sagged as she replaced the receiver. Finally, agonizingly, he saw her face drain of colour as his father's tread could be heard on the stairs. He was still out of sight, but his voice resounded in the hall.

'I think you've got something to tell me, Julie.'

Then he appeared in his dressing-gown, his face and neck still gleaming from the shower.

'Oh Billy, Phil's our son. I had to hear his voice, know he was safe.'

'You did, did you?' Dad's lip curled. It was a smile, but there was no affection or warmth in it.

'This is crazy, Billy. You can't just throw him out on the streets.'

'Don't tell me what I can and can't do, Julie. Don't you dare. Not after all you've done.'

Jamie met his mum's eyes.

'Not in front of Jamie,' she pleaded.

'Maybe the lad should know, find out what his mother's really like. Would you like that, Jamie? Would you like to hear a few home truths about your mum?'

Jamie shrank back.

'Billy, stop it,' said Mum, stepping between them. 'You're frightening him.'

Dad didn't stop. He started to brush past her, and all the time he was saying the same thing, like a war chant. 'Would you like that, son? Hear what your Mum gets up to?'

'Billy!' Mum was shrieking at him.

'Get out of my way,' said Dad, his voice low and hard. 'I want to talk to *my* son.'

But she didn't get out of the way. She stood her ground. Bravely, Jamie thought, though it wasn't the bravery the boys in school talked about, the courage of the streets. She was afraid of his dad. It showed in the way she held her arms in front of her stomach, the way she lowered her head. But she didn't stand aside.

'Please, Billy,' she said. 'Don't do this.'

He stopped and glared at her. It was a look of contempt.

'Billy, don't …'

Then he raised his hand.

'Dad, no!'

Jamie heard the voice. It was like a stranger's, loud and piercing. But he recognized the words as his own.

'Dad, please.'

And it ended right there, with a son's plea to his father.

'You don't deserve a boy like that,' said Dad, lowering his arm and turning on his heel.

Jamie watched him climb the stairs.

'You don't deserve him,' Dad repeated from the landing.

Then Jamie turned towards his mum. He was shaking. 'Are you all right?' he asked.

Mum nodded. But she was shaking too.

Eleven

Last night I ran a risk too many. I said good-night to the lads after a kick-about down the Rec and headed for home over the railway bridge by Cropper Lane. That's where they got me. You must know who I'm talking about. That's right, the un-thinking man's favourite moron, Brain Damage. He had Tez Cronin in tow, but that's not what bothered me. Costello and Jelly Wobble were there. I must be slipping, I didn't even see them coming. They were on top of me before I knew it. Tez got the first punch in, but Costello was the one who was urging everybody on to punch my lights out. As I turned away from Tez, Brain Damage got hold of me and wrenched my head down. Then it was Costello's turn. Up came his knee and I was tasting blood, warm and salty. Then Jelly Wobble had his fingers in my eyes and Costello and Brain Damage were taking free shots.

Brain Damage isn't the kid I turned over so easily last autumn, Costello's seen to that. He's always there, winding evryone up to do me in. I was on a hiding to nothing. Brain Damage was pivoting on his right foot and punching up into my rib cage; hard, shuddering blows that lifted me off my feet. And there was Costello all the time, cheering him on. The first time Brain Damage crossed me, I was able to swat him like a fly. Not any more, not now he'd got Costello pressing his buttons. I was twisting and turning, trying to break free, but Brain Damage was holding on like a bulldog. It was Jelly Wobble who gave me my chance in the end. The fat man was panting and snorting like a pig with sinus trouble, so I decided he was the weak link. I waited until his face was really close then I jerked my head up under his chin. You should have heard him squeal. He'd nearly bitten off his own tongue.

I knew I wasn't going to get a second chance. I dug my elbow into Brain Damage's throat and slapped Costello aside and I was free. Free but not safe.

They were on my heels. I vaulted the safety railings by the railway bridge and scrambled over the gate. There was no game plan. I just had to get away, and the school grounds were as good a place as any. I had this idea the caretaker might come out to see what was causing all the racket. He lives in a house attached to the school building. No such luck. He must have been stuck in front of the TV. I made for the front gate but Jelly Wobble had caught up and he was covering my escape route; Mr Blobby with attitude. I turned to see the gang closing. I'd had it.

'Going somewhere?' sneered Costello.

For once I was lost for words. My heart was playing pat-a-cake with my tonsils. I was in for a hiding.

'Let's sort him,' said Costello.

Brain Damage grinned. He and Tez led the attack. Then I heard something that made my heart sing. It was Jamie shouting from the other side of the road.

'Leave him alone!'

On his own, Jamie wouldn't have made much of a difference. But he wasn't alone, not by a long chalk. There were Ant, Bashir, John and Jimmy. Costello swore under his breath.

'That little blurt again.'

It was his turn to run.

'How did you know I was in trouble?' I panted as my mates scaled the railings.

'We didn't,' said Jamie. 'We'd just knocked off when we saw you going over the fence. We came to investigate.'

'Good job you did,' I said. 'I thought I was dead.'

'Dead jammy,' said Jamie.

'Costello must think you're my minder,' I said. 'He'll really have it in for you.'

Jamie started dancing round, shadow boxing. Like he was Prince Naseem. 'I'll take him. I'll take anybody. I could have been a contender.'

Everybody laughed, even though it wasn't funny. It was a victory laugh, I guess. Only it was all an act on my part. I didn't feel too happy. Costello and Brain Damage had got me in their sights. They wanted me grovelling at their feet. Still, they hadn't got their way yet. What would I do without my mates?

Twelve

Jamie was in high spirits. It gave him a kick, saving Guv's bacon like that. It was nice to see this hard-knock mate of his was human, after all. Guv had always been the wild card. When he first came to the Diamond, he'd had the whole world on his back, and he'd still got by. That's the sort of kid he was, five foot nothing of sheer bottle.

'So what's up with your mum?' asked Ant, breaking in on Jamie's thoughts.

He resented the interruption. 'How do you mean?'

'Uncle Billy was round ours before I came out, and he was calling her for everything. They had a row, or something?'

Jamie hung his head. He was glad the others had gone. He wouldn't have put it past Ant to drag the family's dirty washing out in public. Sensitive, Anthony Glover wasn't. 'Yeah, something like that,' he admitted grudgingly. 'Why, what did he say?'

'I didn't hear it all,' said Ant. 'Mum chased me when she caught me earwigging.' He glanced round, as if anticipating a juicy secret. 'She hasn't got herself another feller, has she?'

Jamie's heart kicked. He scowled, more in misery than in anger. 'Don't be stupid.'

'Why's it stupid? John's mum did.'

'Never!'

'She did. You ask him.'

'So that's why his parents split up?'

'Sounds like it. She wasn't the only one, though. His old man met somebody else, and all.'

Jamie just stared. Not that he cared less about John O'Hara's mum and dad. It was the idea that his might be carrying on like that. Mum? It was just the sort of thing spiteful kids like Costello always picked up on. But his own mother; she couldn't be.

'Dad never said that, did he?'

'What, that she's carrying on? Not in so many words.'

Jamie's heart went cold. 'So what *did* he say? Tell me, Ant.'

Ant was already losing interest in the conversation. 'Oh, he was just mouthing off about something she'd got up to. Don't get your knickers in a twist. I'm just guessing, that's all.'

Ant carried on knocking the ball up as they trailed along South Parade. He was so nonchalant, but his words were like a grenade tossed into Jamie's imagination. Messing around? Mum?

'I don't believe it.'

Ant shrugged his shoulders. 'So don't. It's no skin off

—— 53 ——

my nose. I'm just telling you what I heard. I didn't expect the third degree.'

Jamie dug his hands irritably in his pockets. So what did he expect? The end of South Parade was looming, the parting of the ways.

'Was Dad angry?' asked Jamie.

'He certainly wasn't a happy bunny,' Ant replied off-handedly.

Jamie heard the wind rattling in the Post Office security shutters and suddenly he felt it gnawing the marrow out of his bones. He shivered.

'You OK?' asked Ant.

'Yes, cold, that's all.'

But it was more than the cold. It was the hard, grinding ache of suffering.

Ant gave him a long, cool stare. 'Anyway, I'm off home. St Bede's on Sunday. Remember the last time we met them.'

'Yes, they beat us three–one.'

'And we were lucky to get off that easy. It'll be different this time, though. We're on a roll.'

Jamie was sick at heart. He just wanted Ant to go. 'You reckon?'

'I reckon. See you, Jay.'

'Yeah, see you, Ant.'

As Jamie reached the corner, he found himself thinking about Costello and Brain Damage. Somehow, any time you were feeling low, they just seemed to pop into your head. They could be hanging round the garages, waiting for him. He listened hard, but there wasn't a murmur, nothing but the low, rushing sigh of the wind off the docks. Crashing his foot against the security shutters, Jamie took to his heels, sprinting all the way home, pumping his arms and legs as if the urgent, drumming movement of his body could beat down the awful thoughts that were sweeping through his mind. But they came all the same. She couldn't be, she just couldn't be. If she was, it really would be the end. The hints his dad was always dropping surged through his head relentlessly.

Phil? He's no son of mine.

Try as he might he couldn't ignore them. Jamie reached the front gate and clung to the gatepost. For a moment, it was actually holding him up. All the life had gone out of him. He stared at the open curtains and the illuminated living room beyond. Mum often left them like that until he got in, but that was her. A worry pot. Jamie looked at his house. It seemed so normal from the outside. A home like any other, full of people playing Happy Families. But that's all they were doing, playing. And Guv was always telling him how lucky he was! Jamie caught sight of Mum hovering at the window and waved, but it was a half-hearted gesture. He knew he would have real trouble carrying off the act of normality once he was indoors.

'I'm not late, am I?' he called, shoving the back door open. He said it brightly enough, but it was put on, like the wave.

Mum didn't answer.

'Mum?'

There it was again – the strange panic that always gripped him when she didn't answer. He found her in the living room, still standing looking out on to the darkened street.

'Mum?'

She turned slowly, and that's when he saw it. Running from her ear and along her jaw, almost to the corner of her mouth, a broad, discoloured patch of skin.

'Oh, Mum.'

As he approached her, he noticed that the yellowish skin wasn't half of it. Her throat was heavily bruised, and the line of her jaw was also turning blue.

'Dad?'

She nodded, then hastily qualified her answer. 'It was an accident. The cupboard door ...'

Then the pretence collapsed and she took Jamie in her arms. He felt his face pressed against her and the waves of sobs that shook her.

It was no accident.

PART TWO

Going Missing

One

Jamie was round ours this morning. The moment we were out of earshot of my mum, he went all weepy on me. Talk about embarrassing. If there's one thing I can't handle, it's one of my mates turning on the waterworks. I know it sounds hard, but I just can't cope with it. Crying's for divvies. Ever seen somebody's face when they're crying? Red, quivery and blotchy like a rotten baby. Start wailing and you're just admitting defeat. It's total weakness. OK, yes, I know, Jamie's got something to cry about. I'd never have had his dad down as someone who knocks his wife about, but it seems that's what he's been doing.

'So what started it?' I asked.

'Dunno,' said Jamie. 'All I know is, it's got something to do with our Phil.'

I didn't know what he was getting at so I just looked back expectantly.

'I never told you, did I?' Jamie mumbled eventually. 'Dad's thrown Phil out.'

'What, last night?'

'No, three weeks ago.'

I was gobsmacked. How had he kept something like that to himself so long? Here he was, the kid I envied, and he'd been through the mill just like me. It turns out there's been a civil war going on in Jamie's house since year dot.

'And you never told me?' I complained. 'I thought I was your best mate.'

'You are.'

Then he started telling me everything. Seems Jamie's been his dad's blue-eyed boy since, well, forever. Billy Moore always had it in for Phil. Jamie says he was always aware of it, even when he was dead little, the way his dad was so cold towards Phil. He still doesn't understand it, but he knows it's the thing that's behind all the rows.

'I bet you hate your old man,' I said. I'd have hated mine.

Jamie shook his head. 'I think it's her fault as much as his,' he told me, so quiet I could hardly hear him.

That didn't ring true, somehow. I mean, let's be real, who was hitting who?

'How do you work that out?' I asked, really annoyed with him. The way I felt, he could have been talking about my mum. How come it's always the woman who gets dumped on, anyway?

Jamie started to say something, then the shutters came down. I could guess what he was feeling. Anger. With himself, with them. It's a road I've been down. He wasn't about to open up any more, though. He'd said too much already. 'I can't tell you,' he said.

'Fair enough,' I answered, a bit nettled. 'It's your business. But what are you going to do?'

'What can I do?' said Jamie.

His face was puffy, like a baby's. Weak. I could hardly look at him.

'What can I do?' he asked again, all whingey and pathetic.

I didn't know, but I'm sure of one thing. If this goes on it's going to affect Jamie's form again, just when we've got him back on the rails. I mean, it's St Bede's tomorrow, our chance to climb well away from the bottom of the table, and this trouble at Jamie's house is bound to screw things up for us. I bet you think I'm really tight on Jamie. I'm not, I know he's more than just our striker, and I know what it's like to hurt inside. I've had a lifetime of it. That doesn't mean I'm going to crack open another box of Kleenex, though. What does he expect – a weepy party? If there's one

—— 60 ——

thing Jamie doesn't need right now, it's someone egging him on to turn wimp.

You know what you do when somebody kicks you in the teeth? Bite his foot off, that's what. You've got to fight back, that's what I told Jamie. I don't know if he will, mind. He just looked at me with these big, doggy eyes like he expected me to put my arms round him or something.

Dream on, Jay. I'm not the shoulder-to-cry-on type. What you need right now is a bit of backbone.

Two

'Don't let them get to you.'

Kev bridled at Jamie's advice.

'I'm not.'

'Pull the other one, Guv, it's got bells on.'

They both had their eyes on Brain Damage's little crew lined up on the touch-line. It was a real cockroach chorus. Only it wasn't really Brain Damage's gang any more. He was the front man, the muscle, but it was Costello who was pulling the strings.

'This is new,' observed Bashir, jockeying with his marker as he waited for Jimmy to take the throw-in. 'They've never dared come down to the match before.'

Jamie glanced at Kev. He recognized the tell-tale twitch in his friend's temple, a sure sign of anger – and being rattled.

'They never had Costello before,' said Kev.

'Try to forget about them,' Jamie advised.

It was easier said than done. Jimmy's throw found Kev, but he fluffed his flick-on, giving possession to St Bede's.

'Nice one, Guv,' chortled Tez Cronin.

'Hang on a minute, Tez,' said Brain Damage in his best mocking voice. 'Isn't McGovern supposed to be playing for the other side?'

'No-o-o,' gasped Tez in mock amazement.

Costello didn't say a word. His silence was hanging over Kev like a sword on a thread.

'I'm going to kill them,' snarled Kev.

'I'd rather we stuffed this lot first,' said Ratso, indicating the blue-shirted St Bede's players who were besieging Daz's goal.

'And keep your temper,' called Dave. 'Disciplinary points, remember.'

'Who does he think he is?' mused Kev, watching Dave jog away. 'My guardian angel, or something?'

'I don't know,' said Jamie. 'But he's right. Keep a lid on your temper.'

Darting an angry glance at the boys on the touch-line, Kev set off towards the Diamonds' penalty area. It was a hard-fought match. St Bede's were the wingless wonders of the South Sefton Junior League. They packed the mid-field and doubled up on the opposition danger men. They were proving almost impossible to break down.

'My ball,' bellowed Daz, flying off his line to gather St Bede's lofted cross.

But Gord had already gone up for it. The team-mates collided, leaving the centre to drop dangerously into the goal-mouth. Spotting the threat to the goal, Kev threw himself at the ball.

One of the St Bede's lads went for it at the same time and knocked Kev off balance. Struggling to keep on his feet, Kev succeeded only in lashing it against his own crossbar. It was a red-faced and desperately relieved Diamonds' skipper who picked himself up off the floor.

'Close,' shouted Brain Damage. 'That was a good effort, McGovern.'

'Yeah,' added Costello, 'Pity it was your own goal.'

That set off another gale of exaggerated laughter.

'I'd like to see you do better,' snapped Kev. 'Anyway, I thought you played for Blessed Hearts.'

'I used to,' said Costello. 'Since I moved up here I've been looking for a new side to join.' His eyes twinkled mischievously. 'What about this outfit of yours?'

'Over my dead body,' said Kev.

'I'm sure that can be arranged,' chuckled Costello. 'What do you reckon, Andy?'

Brain Damage nodded. Like a ventriloquist's dummy.

Kev stamped away, shaking his head.

'I've told you, haven't I?' said Jamie, 'They're not worth bothering about. Just try to shut them out.'

Kev gave him a sideways look. 'You must be feeling better,' he said. 'Giving me advice like this.'

The corner of Jamie's mouth twitched. Kev was wrong. He was finding life pretty hard to take.

'So it's still going on?' asked Kev.

Jamie ran his hand nervously over his hair. 'What do you think? I was awake half the night, thinking about it. Anyway, forget about my troubles. We've a game to win.'

Kev nodded and threw himself back into the fray. It wasn't long before he started showing a bit of the old steel, dispossessing the gangling St Bede's striker on the edge of his own penalty area. Dribbling skilfully out of defence, he picked out Bashir with a well-crafted cross-field pass. He gave Costello a long, hard look.

'Quiet now, aren't you?' he hissed.

Costello looked away.

Meanwhile on the field, Bashir took the ball in his stride and hit it hard and low into the area.

Dave and Jamie dived simultaneously, but it eluded both of them.

'Nicely-worked move,' shouted Ronnie encouragingly. 'Play up lads, it's nearly half-time.'

The next attack started with a blistering run out of defence by Jimmy. His pace and close control left the challenging St Bede's defender for dead.

'Cross it, Jimmy,' cried Dave. 'Knock it over. Come on, Jim, first time.'

Jimmy obliged, his looping ball heading for the near post. As Dave made his run, Jamie smiled. It had goal written all over it. Dave didn't disappoint. Dropping his head slightly, he met it a glancing blow with his forehead, guiding it delicately past the St Bede's keeper.

One–nil.

St Bede's didn't fold, though. They came back with a couple of stirring attacks, but at the half-time whistle the Diamonds remained one up.

'This isn't over yet, you know,' said Ronnie as his players flopped on the grass. 'These lads have got a lot about them. You're going to have to keep this really tight.'

Nobody was arguing.

'I can't believe it's only half-time,' groaned John. 'I'm whacked.'

'Well, thank you for that really important observation, Mr Positive,' said Ratso.

Everybody laughed. Except John, of course.

'Seriously though,' said Ronnie. 'They're going to come out fired up. Don't underestimate them.'

Jamie peered round. He knew exactly what Kev

would be doing. Sure enough, he was keeping an eye on Costello and Brain Damage.

'I don't like it,' said Kev. 'They've never come on my turf before. They're getting too rotten cocky for my liking.' He noticed Jamie staring into space. 'Are you listening to me?'

'Sorry,' said Jamie. 'I was thinking about Mum and Dad.'

'What about them?' came a voice. It was Ant.

'Oh, nothing,' said Jamie.

'Suit yourself,' said Ant. 'Come on, we're starting again.'

'What was that about?' asked Kev, as they jogged back on to the field.

'I don't want Ant to know too much,' said Jamie. 'He's always on my dad's side.'

'And you?'

Jamie thought for a moment. 'I'm on nobody's side.' He wondered if that was true. He felt sorry for Mum, so sorry part of him really hated his dad. She was the one who got hit, after all. But what if she *was* messing about? Wouldn't that make things different? 'I'm just piggy-in-the-middle,' he added.

Ronnie's second-half prediction was proved correct right from the re-start. St Bede's were buzzing round the Diamonds' box like wasps round jam. First a raking shot then a close-range header tested Daz.

'Hello,' he raged, going round tapping his knuckles on his defenders' heads. 'Anybody in? Forgotten how to defend, have you?'

'Shut it,' said Ant. 'You do your job and we'll do ours.'

'Oh yeah?' Daz retorted. 'Like when?'

As if to answer Daz's question, Ant rose to meet the

St Bede's corner and headed it clear out of the penalty area.

'Now that's more like it,' said Daz approvingly.

Ant glared. He knew the ranting and raving was all Daz's way of staying focussed, but some of his barbs really got through to his team-mates. Unfortunately, Jamie had gone walkabout, so John had to collect the long header. He shook off his marker then drove forward. He found himself in acres of space.

Ronnie glared at Jamie. He'd had one good game but he just wasn't consistent. Then he turned his attention to what was happening further upfield. 'Run it, John!' yelled Ronnie. 'Take them on.'

The last St Bede's defender lunged at John, the sort of rash tackle that could cripple you, but John hurdled the flailing legs at full tilt. He had only the goalie to beat.

Steadying himself, he feinted left then slid it under the keeper's body. As the ball slapped the net, he wheeled away in a victory run. He wasn't the only one to celebrate, but Kev had his own target. He dived full length on the turf, right in front of Costello and his cronies.

'Gone a bit quiet, haven't you?' asked Kev.

'Shut it, McGovern,' said Tez.

'Why don't you come and shut it for me?' said Kev.

Tez didn't look too thrilled at the prospect. Costello and Brain Damage were undaunted, though. They still had something in reserve.

'Tell him your news,' said Costello.

Brain Damage smiled. 'I don't know what you've got to smile about, McGovern,' he said, then, with a brutal flourish. 'Not when your old man's in nick.'

Kev stood up. The words had jerked him to his feet. 'What are you on about?'

Brain Damage looked so smug. He let Kev stew for a few seconds before continuing. 'He got lifted outside his flat this morning. Our Lee told me.'

'This is a wind-up, right?'

Another smirk. 'Think what you want.'

With that, Brain Damage winked at Costello and they led the gang towards Jacob's Lane. By way of a parting shot, he turned and called: 'What do you reckon, Guv? Take a guess. Am I telling the truth or not?'

The match finished up three–nil, with Jimmy Mintoe scrambling home the final goal. Kev hardly noticed. He was even too preoccupied to notice that Ronnie had substituted Jamie. The pair of them ended the game as spectators.

Three

I disappeared straight after the match. The whistle was still in the ref's mouth when I took off down Jacob's Lane. I didn't even say goodbye to Jamie. It's funny, you know, sometimes on these programmes on TV they try to show the way you think. Like when the detective sees something in his mind's eye and bingo, he realizes who the murderer is. You see inside somebody's head, and it's just like a re-run of the world outside, crystal clear. But your mind isn't like that at all. It's a blizzard of thoughts and memories, all swirling round. As I ran down South Parade towards home, I was dizzy with my thoughts.

I saw my dad, slumped on a bench in a police cell, and Lee Ramage in his BMW cruising the estate. I even found myself wondering if Lee had set Dad up. I wouldn't put anything past that family. There was me sitting on Dad's shoulders when I was about four, watching the ferry chugging across the river, and me not long after in the back of the car, swallowing my fear. That was the night Dad torched a warehouse down by the docks. Then there was Mum telling me I had to forget him, and her face red with crying because he'd left us. Every memory crowded in on me, like little kids round an ice-cream van, and they all wanted my attention. But not one of them would wait in line.

My whole life was coming at me in bits and all these little bits shouting and screaming, telling me this was the part that really mattered. I even found thoughts of Jamie popping into my head. I'd cleared off without a word and I knew how miserable he was. The way he was playing, for a start. He'd always been lethal, a baby-faced assassin. But things at home had ruined his game. He wasn't half the kid he used to be. A few more games like the one against St Bede's and Ronnie would be looking for another striker. I couldn't get Jamie's face out of my mind, even when it was full of my dad. I'd seen the downcast eyes and the shattered expression. It looks like we're two of a kind. Life's giving us both the run-around.

By the time I reached the back door I was choking on my own breath.

'What's wrong?' asked Mum when I burst into the living room. 'Whatever's the matter?'

And it all came out, what Brain Damage had said and how I was scared and I wanted to know he was all right. Well, Mum was brilliant. She got on the phone to my nan. You know, Dad's mum, the one I never see, because Mum's always got an excuse to keep me away. It turned out Dad had been released half an hour earlier after questioning. It was about beating up those fellers from Bootle. What about Lee Ramage, I told Mum to ask, but *no, my nan didn't know anything about him, just the good news that they weren't going to hold my dad.*

Then Mum hung up and put her hand on my shoulder. 'He's playing a dangerous game, your dad.'

I nodded. She didn't need to tell me that. I wasn't stupid. I knew exactly how risky Dad's life was. In fact I probably had a better idea than Mum did, but I kept that to myself.

'You can see why I worry about you, son,' she went on. 'I don't want you thinking what your dad does is big or something.'

But by then I wasn't really listening. I was so relieved I went upstairs and cried my eyes out. Yes, that's right. Me, the tough guy. The friend who didn't feel a shred of sympathy when Jamie was hurting. Still, Dad was out and he was in the clear, and that's all that mattered.

Four

'All right, Jay, long time no see.'

The tall seventeen-year-old was the last person Jamie had expected to meet at the school gates.

'Phil!'

Phil smiled. 'You haven't forgotten me, then?'

Jamie glanced uneasily behind him. Costello and Brain Damage were paying close attention to the brothers' reunion. There was enough curiosity to kill a hundred cats.

'Not here, Phil. Let's take a walk.'

Phil followed Jamie's eyes and frowned. 'So what's the matter with those two?'

'What do you think? That's Brain Damage Ramage you're talking about.'

'Of course. Young Andrew always was a bit of a scally.'

Jamie nodded. 'And that's his new mate. Luke Costello. He's even worse.'

'Jay, hang on for me.' The shout came from Kev. He'd been kept back in class by Jacko. A word in the shell-like over some smart-Alec comment in class.

Jamie waited uncomfortably for Kev to make his way through the jostling crowds at the gates. He was careful not to meet the probing eyes of Costello and Brain Damage, but he knew Phil's return was being meticulously recorded. That's the way Costello was. Everything mentally filed for future use. Jamie was starting to realize why Kev thought his arrival was such a big deal.

'You weren't going without me, were you?' asked Kev. That's when he noticed Phil. 'Hi Phil. Long time no see.'

'I don't mean to be rude, Kevin,' said Phil, 'But I need a word with Jamie in private.'

Kev nodded. 'I'll do my disappearing act. Catch you later, Jay. See you, Phil.'

'Yes, see you.'

Phil watched Kev weaving his way through the departing children. 'Isn't he the lad Mum and Dad told you not to knock around with?'

Jamie nodded. 'They've eased up a bit. I think they know he's not as bad as everybody makes out.'

Phil smiled. He looked non-commital. 'Come on, let's get a coffee.'

'I'd better not. Mum'll be worried if I'm late.'

'I was there earlier. She knows I'm meeting you.'

Jamie's eyes widened. 'You went round the house! But what if Dad came home early?'

'He's in Preston installing machinery. That's why I chose today.'

Jamie dug his hands in his pockets and kept pace with Phil. As they crossed the dual carriageway towards South Parade, he was still aware of Costello's interest. He certainly hadn't forgiven Jamie for the fight outside the community centre.

'What do you want?' asked Phil as they joined the queue in Sayers.

'Sprite … and a ring doughnut.'

Jamie felt uneasy about the meeting, but he wasn't going to pass up the offer of something to eat.

'A milky coffee, a Sprite and a ring doughnut,' Phil told the waitress.

Jamie followed him to a table by the window.

'Where are you living?' he asked.

'I've got a flat with friends. Sheil Road way.'

'So you've been just up the road all the time.'

'That's right. I dossed on floors for a few days, then I heard about this box-room in a student house. It's a good job. For a while I was thinking I'd end up selling *The Big Issue*.'

Jamie winced. He'd thought of that when Phil first went missing. He'd dragged Kev round town the Saturday afternoon after he left, clocking the *Big Issue* vendors. Kev hadn't cottoned on, though. He thought they were pricing new trainers.

'You could have let us know,' Jamie scolded.

'I told my mates not to let on. I wanted the dust to settle. You know what Dad's like.'

Jamie lowered his eyes. It was easy for Phil. Everything was painted in black and white. To him Dad was an ogre. Full stop, end of story.

'It's been tough, has it?'

Jamie nodded. 'He's been knocking her about. But you'll know that.'

Phil leant back in his chair. 'I've seen the evidence with my own eyes. What a pig.'

'Phil, why are you back?'

'I've got to get Mum to leave him.'

Jamie's senses reeled. 'You're joking.'

'You've seen her face.'

'She's done things too.' There, Jamie had said it. Only he felt lousy the moment the words were out of his mouth. It was like he'd dragged a cheese grater over his heart.

Phil planted his elbows on the table and leant forward, suddenly hostile. 'Run that by me again.'

Jamie was squirming. Even the words were an act of betrayal. 'It's something Dad keeps saying. And Ant.'

Phil shook his head. 'I don't believe this. There she is with a face like a punch-ball and you're listening to *his* poison.'

'But what if she is ...?' Jamie couldn't bring himself to say it.

'Is what?' demanded Phil angrily.

'Messing around.'

'Is that what he's been saying? What a rotten lousy pig.'

Jamie stared miserably at the doughnut. Suddenly he didn't feel a bit hungry.

'And Ant's telling the same story?'

Jamie nodded.

'Then the old man's spreading it all round the family. He's getting people to take sides against Mum, that's what he's doing.'

Jamie found himself looking away, out into the Parade, but there was no respite there either.

He saw Costello standing with Tez and Brain Damage across the road. They obviously thought there was mileage in Phil's return.

'You don't think it's true then, what Dad's saying?'

'Of course it isn't. Mum's never so much as looked at another feller. That's her trouble. I just wish she had.'

'Phil!'

'Well, it's true. There's loyal and there's crazy and she's gone to Hell and back. It's all right for you, Jay. You've had it easy. It's me and Mum who've always had to take it off him.'

'But why?'

'Why do you think?' said Phil. 'Because he's a flaming lunatic. It's about time you realized; he's got a slate loose.'

'He's always treated me OK,' Jamie answered sulkily.

'Well, bully for you,' snapped Phil. 'Is that all that matters to you, Jamie? Doesn't it bother you that he kicks Mum all round the floor?'

'Don't exaggerate!'

'So what's that on her face, Jay, blackcurrant juice?' Phil was snarling out the words, heavy on the sarcasm. 'Or maybe she's been trying out the face paints. Funny, I thought it was a big, ugly bruise.'

'I mean he doesn't do it all the time.'

Phil's eyes narrowed. 'You mean you think he doesn't.'

Jamie returned his look. 'I don't—'

'Don't you get it, Jay? He's been at it for years. Just verbal stuff most of the time, making her feel rotten about herself, running her down. She thinks she's ugly and stupid. That's right, our lovely mum. Ugly and stupid. That's what he's done to her. But even that isn't enough for the old beggar. He's even worse sometimes.'

'How do you mean, worse?'

'Pushing, shoving, kicks and punches sometimes.'

Phil waited for this to sink in.

'That's right, what you've seen wasn't a one-off. It's been going on for years. You were too young to understand, but she's had the marks to prove it. Loads of times.'

'But why didn't I know?'

Phil shook his head. 'She was trying to protect you.' He gave a bitter laugh. 'She's good with the make-up, too.'

Jamie still didn't see Dad the way Phil did, but he also felt he'd let Mum down, and he felt rotten on both accounts.

'Do you remember my fourteenth birthday party, when she fell against the back door?'

'Yes, why?'

'She didn't fall.'

'You mean that was Dad?'

Phil nodded. 'There's plenty more. Her swollen wrist last Boxing Day. The fall she had in Benidorm. Fall, my foot! The only thing she fell on was his fist. Do you want me to go on?'

Jamie shook his head.

'Sick, isn't it? It's getting worse, and all. She's got to walk out.'

Jamie's stomach clenched. 'You want them to split up?'

'What's to split up? You can't call that a marriage. For crying out loud, Jamie, for Mum life's a living nightmare.'

Jamie stood up suddenly. He was trembling. He felt that he was burning inside. 'Stop it, Phil.'

Phil must have realized he'd gone to far because he began to speak more softly. 'Sit down, Jay.'

'Only if you say it's not true.'

'Sorry,' said Phil. 'But it's true, all right.'

'It can't be that bad, Phil. It can't!'

Jamie turned and fell against the neighbouring table. The old dear started to protest but he carried on making his escape, knocking chairs aside and barging past the other customers to a chorus of 'Young lout' and 'Kids, no respect.'

'Jamie,' shouted Phil, giving chase. 'Hang on. I don't want you running off like this.'

But Jamie had got to the door and he wasn't about to turn back. Home was out. Dad wouldn't be back until after six and Phil might turn up there. He thought of Kev. By the time he'd made it to the corner Phil was at the door of the café.

'Jamie, come back!'

Jamie didn't even check his stride. He didn't want to hear any more and he wasn't going to. He didn't care what Phil said, he wasn't about to let his family fall apart. If he ran fast enough, he could leave it all behind him. And that's what he did.

He fled, past the last-minute shoppers, past an intrigued Costello and a gawking Brain Damage, shutting it all out.

He just ran.

Five

I've just had Jamie round. He wasn't half upset. I've never seen him like that. I'm beginning to understand just how bad things are round his house. Weird, isn't it, you think you know somebody then you discover they've been living this hidden life all the time. I'd always thought our families were so different. Suddenly I find out we've more in common than I could have dreamt. We've both got parents pulling in opposite directions, and it's us that get ripped apart.

To tell you the truth, I feel rotten about Jamie's visit. I really wish I hadn't told him anything. But I did, and I've been worrying about it ever since he left. Jamie says Phil wants to split the family up. That's his way of telling me his mum's thinking of getting out from under. You know my problem? I'm OK fighting my own battles, but when it comes to other people I say the most stupid things. I told Jamie what I thought he wanted to hear. I'm sitting there opposite him and he's fixing me with these pleading eyes. Then he pops the question: You think they should stay together, don't you, Guv? You don't like your Mum and Dad living apart, do you? *And like the sap I am, I tell him families should stay together. Kev the Agony Uncle. There's only one problem; the advice stank.*

Just think about it, Jamie's dad's been battering his mum. And from what Jamie's told me, he very nearly put her in hospital this time. Even my dad's never done anything like that. He saves his fists for business. *So what do I tell Jamie? Try to keep them together, that's what. Brilliant, eh? Just to keep him happy. You know what, much as I love him, if Dad dared lift a finger to Mum I'd want to cut his heart out. Honest I would.*

There's something else that's been playing on my mind, and all. A really mean, selfish thing it is, too. Jamie's played two stinkers on the run, and that's got me more worried than anything. We're nearly there, you see. A couple of weeks and we're in the Cup semi-final. We've drawn Ajax Aintree, top of the table and the strongest outfit in our league. They beat us seven–three the last time they played us. It's the most important game we've played in. So what has to happen? This thing with Jamie's dad, that's what. It's setting Jamie and Ant against each other. Sure, it's just a bit of the verbal up to now, but it's getting worse. I've been noticing it for a while. Ant keeps saying things, repeating what he's heard off his Uncle Billy. Well, you can imagine what that does to Jamie. I really feel for him. He loves his dad, but he won't have his mum slagged off either, and that's all Ant seems to do. The whole family seems to have it in for Jamie's mum. I can see there being a real bust-up over this.

So there's another reason for the advice I gave Jamie. Keep the family together and you keep the Diamonds together. At least that's what I was thinking half the time. I was also thinking what a louse I was that I couldn't help Jamie out of his misery. I can't, though. Maybe with my history, I'm scared of getting too involved. It's like the weaker I feel on the inside, the harder I act on the outside. I don't know what's going to happen. Once things start falling apart, it's never easy to put them back together. I'm an expert, remember. Poor Jamie. He really thinks that if his parents stay together things will be hunky-dory.

Sorry, Jamie lad, but those kind of dreams just don't come true.

Six

'So what went on between you and Phil?'

Mum met Jamie on the doorstep. She seemed tense and angry. 'And what do you mean by staying out till this time? I've been worried sick.'

Jamie shrugged. The gesture owed more to defiance than anything else.

'Oh, get in here.'

She tugged at his sleeve and almost ran him into the living room. 'And what's this about me *messing around*?'

The questions were coming thick and fast. Jamie felt overwhelmed.

'Well, you said enough to Phil. Haven't you got anything to say to me?'

Jamie just stared at her. He was numb. He wasn't scared or worried any more, just exhausted.

'Jamie, I'm talking to you.'

'Where's my dad?'

Mum's eyes narrowed to a squint. 'Is that all you care about?'

One look at her bruised jaw and Jamie regretted his question.

'If you must know, he's gone round his sister's.'

Mum couldn't bring herself to say Aunty Irene's name. She was obviously as aware as Jamie that the Moores were ganging up on her.

'You been arguing?' asked Jamie.

'No, not really.' Mum ran her hands through her hair. 'We don't talk enough to argue.'

The words hit Jamie's stomach like a fist.

'Anyway,' Mum continued, 'Come and sit down by me. I want to know what's going on in that mind of yours.'

Jamie hovered uncertainly in front of her.

'Come on, son, sit down. It's time we talked.'

'Has Phil gone?'

'Ages ago. He wasn't going to risk a confrontation with your dad.'

Jamie sat down. 'Mum, what's it all about?'

'Don't you know already?'

Jamie nodded. 'Some of it.'

'And I dare say you've been making the rest up. With a little help from *his* side of the family.' She fairly spat out the last few words.

'So what's your dad been spreading round about me?'

Jamie coloured. 'I don't want to —'

'It's all right, Jamie, I can guess. You don't have to be on Mastermind to know what's going on in your dad's head.'

Jamie's flesh was creeping. If she said there was nothing to it, he knew he wouldn't be able to believe her. And if there was ... It didn't bear thinking about.

'He says I've got another feller. That's it, isn't it?'

Jamie nodded. 'That's what Ant said.'

Mum glared. 'Anthony did! So Billy's bad-mouthing me to kids now.'

'We've had a couple of arguments about it.'

Mum softened. 'So you stood up for me, did you?'

Jamie smiled thinly. Not enough, he thought to himself.

'Anything else?'

'Just this thing Dad always says.'

He paused, but Mum's eyes were on him, pressing him to explain.

Jamie drew a deep breath. 'That Phil isn't his son.'

Some things you wish you could un-say, but Jamie knew that had become impossible.

Mum took his hand. 'None of it's true, son, if that's what you've been wondering.'

'Then why does he say it?' Jamie cried.

'Your dad's the most jealous man I've ever met,' said Mum. 'He's a fool to himself. For as long as I've known him he's driven himself mad over things.'

'Why, though?'

'There doesn't have to be a reason,' said Mum. 'Before I met your dad, I used to go out with this lad, Tommy McCann. We worked together at the BAT. I stopped seeing him when I got engaged to Billy.

Anyway, the factory was shutting down so we had a works night out. You know, just to say good-bye before we went our different ways. Anyway, the DJ was putting on a few smoochy numbers near the end, so Tommy asked me for a dance. It was *only* a dance, but when your dad came to pick me up he saw us together. He went crazy. He tackled Tommy about it and there was a fight.'

'You mean Dad and this Tommy?'

Mum nodded. 'They took some separating. After that he never would let go of it. I thought he'd just forget about it, but he didn't. We got married and Phil came along, but your dad had got it in his head somehow that Phil was Tommy's kid. I couldn't move out of the house after that. Billy wouldn't let me out unless he was with me. I couldn't even go on a girls' night out with my mates. It's mad. I've only ever loved your dad.'

'Loved?'

Mum smiled. 'Maybe I do still love him, but this ... I can't go on living in fear, Jamie. Phil's right. I've put up with the bullying long enough. He's hurt me once too often. I'm still young. I can't just throw my life away.'

Jamie felt the old rush of panic. 'But you're married.'

'Your dad doesn't seem to think about that.'

Jamie went quiet.

'You'll still have us both, Jamie. Just not together in the same house.'

Jamie's eyes were prickling and his voice was thick with emotion. 'Have you told Dad?'

'Not yet. I don't know if I dare.'

'Then what are you going to do?'

Mum leant forward. 'Not a word of this to your dad.'

'What is it, Mum?'

'Phil's sorted out a flat for us, nothing much, but at

least it's somewhere. Just until we can decide how to handle this.'

'But I don't want a flat,' cried Jamie. 'I want to stay here. I want you and Dad.'

'And you can still have us. But not together. That's over, Jamie.'

Jamie felt as if he was drowning. He thought he'd prepared himself for the worst, but this was beyond even that.

'Oh Mum, it can't be.'

Mum slowly stroked her bruised jaw.

'It has to be.'

Seven

Three days went by and Jamie didn't tell.

He went on another fishing trip to Wright's pool, but he still held his tongue. And in the car to and from ju-jitsu. And sitting in front of the television watching the FA Cup fifth-round replay. Not a word. He wore his silence like a second skin, and for every minute of silence he hated himself more.

Things came to a head the Saturday evening after his heart-to-heart with Mum. He'd been in bed about half an hour when he heard the sounds downstairs. At first it was just raised voices. Nothing unusual about that, thought Jamie. Quiet conversation – now that would have been really out of the ordinary! Soon after, the dull, thudding sound began, and the screams. He tried to shut them out, burying his head in his pillow, but nothing could stop them.

'Billy, don't!'

Mum's cry crashed inside Jamie's skull. He couldn't just lie there.

'Billy!'

This cry was louder, more afraid. Jamie knew he had to do something. He ran to the top of the stairs and stopped. What *could* he do? Feeling his stomach turn over, he began to walk downstairs. And all the while he kept hearing the same phrase from his dad. *A little birdy*.

'How do I know?' he heard his dad bawling. 'A little birdy told me.'

'Mum, are you all right?'

It was Dad who answered.

'Get to bed, son.'

'I want to see Mum.'

'Your dad's right,' came her voice. 'Go back up.'

Jamie reached the living-room door. An armchair had been turned over and there was a broken vase on the carpet. He edged forward.

'A little birdy,' his dad repeated sourly. 'At least I've got one friend. It's the only way I know anything.'

That's when he saw them. Mum was half sitting, half lying on the carpet with Dad standing over her. His fists were clenched and he was red in the face, panting like a dog.

'Leave her alone,' begged Jamie.

'I thought I told you to get to bed,' his dad replied. 'This is none of your business.'

'Please, Dad.'

'Are you going to do what I say?'

Jamie was frightened, but the fear didn't stop him. 'Not if you're going to hit her.'

Dad took a long, hard look at Jamie, then stepped away from Mum. 'So that's the way it is. She's poisoned you against me, too.'

'No, Dad, I just want you to stop.'

'Stop,' said Dad. 'I haven't even started.'

'Please, Billy,' begged Mum. 'Not in front of Jamie.'

'Shut it,' snapped Dad. 'I've heard all I needed from my little birdy.'

'Bill, you're not making sense.'

'No? Well, my little birdy is. Singing out the truth, that's my little birdy.'

Jamie moved towards his mother and knelt beside her.

Dad shook his head. 'I'm going out.'

Jamie watched him take his leather jacket from the peg in the hallway.

'I just don't want you to hurt her,' he said.

Dad shook his head. 'You shouldn't have interfered, Jamie.'

Then he was gone.

'What did he mean, Mum, about the little birdy?'

Mum looked away. 'I don't know, son. He isn't making sense.'

Jamie watched her rising painfully to her feet.

'Come on, Jamie,' she said as the car started up. 'Pack some clothes. We're going.'

'Now?' asked Jamie. 'But we can't.'

Mum gingerly felt her ribs. 'We have to. He hurt me this time, Jamie, really hurt me.'

Jamie saw the way she was holding herself and he knew there was no point arguing. They had to go.

Eight

I knew something was up when Jamie didn't turn up at school. I caught Ant at break and asked if he knew why.

*After a few minutes of surly stares he finally spilt the beans.
Jamie had gone. That knocked me back, I can tell you. My
best mate. Gone. Even then Ant wasn't finished. He started
slagging off Jamie's mum. He was calling her all sorts. I
knew he must have heard it at home, but it was no excuse. I
couldn't just stand there while he bad-mouthed her. It
almost felt as if he was taking a pop at* my *mum. It turned
into quite a row, Ant hurling abuse at Jamie and his mum
and me defending them. I didn't care what Ant thought. I
knew exactly what Jamie was going through. I know what
it's like standing in no-man's land while your parents tear
lumps out of each other. It's scary and lonely and most of
all it hurts. It's a game you just can't win.*

*In the end I must have gone too far, because Ant really
flipped. One more word and I could stuff my stupid team.
I'd be sorry, Ant promised. I drew a deep sigh. I already
was.*

Nine

Jamie woke early to the sound of church bells. It took a
moment or two for his mind to clear. Then he was
awake and looking up at a dingy ceiling criss-crossed
with hairline cracks. Suddenly there was an emptiness
inside him that nothing would fill. He winced, thinking
of the neat artexing his father had done in his own
bedroom.

'Mum?'

She stirred in the single divan bed across the room.

'What is it, Jamie?'

'What's the time?'

'About seven, son. Can't you sleep?'

Jamie sat up and examined the sleeping arrangements. He'd had to bed down on a lumpy mattress on the floor.

'Not really.'

'This bed isn't very comfortable either.'

'It's not that.'

Mum turned and looked at him. 'I know.'

'What do you think my dad's doing?'

Mum sighed. 'I'm past caring.'

'You don't mean that.'

She ran her hands through her hair. 'Don't be so sure, Jamie.'

Jamie flopped back on to the mattress, weighed down by an overwhelming sense of hopelessness. He listened to the church bells. It was Sunday. The Diamonds would be waking up in their own beds, ready for the match with Ajax Aintree.

'We're playing the league leaders today,' he said. He'd choked on the words a couple of times before he managed to say them. Somehow he didn't care how insensitive he sounded. He had to talk about his mates.

'You don't think you're playing, do you?' Mum demanded. She was sitting up too, pulling a dressing-gown over her shoulders.

Jamie began to mumble guiltily. 'I don't know ... I thought ...'

'Well, whatever it was, you can unthink it. That'll be the first place your dad will look.'

'But we can't hide forever!'

'Who said anything about forever? I need time to sort myself out. This is a big step, Jamie. I can't face your dad yet. I just can't.'

'So I can't see my mates?'

The idea of missing the Ajax game gnawed at Jamie's insides. The league game would be a vital warm-up for the two sides' clash in the Challenge Cup semi-final. The first of their two meetings in a fortnight.

'If it means Billy tracing me through you, then the answer's no. I'll be in touch with the school as well. You can have a few days off while I get my head together.'

'But it isn't fair,' cried Jamie. 'You can't just lock me away in here.'

Mum swung her legs to the floor and leant forward. 'I know this is tough, but I've got no choice.'

Jamie saw the bruising on her face, but he couldn't bring himself to back off. 'Why can't we stay at my gran's then?' he asked. 'It'd be better than this dump.'

Mum was exasperated. 'How many times do I have to explain, Jamie? We can't stay with anyone your dad knows. Not the way he is. I've got to lie low until he finally sees that we're finished. Your gran and grandad understand that. I just wish you would.'

Jamie understood, but understanding isn't accepting. You don't live nearly twenty years of your life with somebody then walk away without a murmur.

'What if you talked it over with him?'

Mum tossed her head back and gave a bitter laugh. 'Talk? Don't you think I've tried?'

'So you mean it's over?'

'Yes it's over.'

'But he's my dad.'

Jamie could feel his mum's eyes on him. He knew what she was thinking. What did she have to say to make him understand? But he did understand. He knew she was right. He knew she'd had to leave, just like he knew she had to hide herself away. But there are things bigger and deeper than just knowing something in your head, and walking out on Dad *felt* all wrong.

'I know this is tough on you,' she began, her voice softer and more understanding. 'But I couldn't stay.'

Jamie could feel the early morning chill on his bare shoulders and the ache of loss throbbing inside him.

'I know, Mum, but this is horrible.'

'The flat, you mean? We won't be here long. I haven't got the money even if I wanted to.'

Jamie shook his head. 'Not the flat, Mum. Things falling apart.'

His mind was full of the things that mattered to him. His mates, the belongings that littered his bedroom, the Diamonds. They started as vivid pictures. Then just when they were real enough to touch they began to fade. Like ghosts.

'I'm sorry, Jamie, but I had to do this. There was no other way. I had no choice.'

Jamie looked around at their cheap, gloomy surroundings.

Nor did he.

Ten

'I knew he wouldn't show,' snorted Ant. 'Too ashamed, I'll bet.'

Kev was in no mood for Ant's sniping. 'Just leave it.'

The rest of the team were watching the encounter. They were looking really uncomfortable.

'You heard what Guv said,' Gord ventured. 'Jamie hasn't been in touch.'

But Ant wasn't satisfied. 'And you believe him?'

The antagonism between Kev and Ant had been growing for days, but Kev hadn't expected it to come to a head so quickly.

'Hang on a minute, Ant. Are you calling me a liar?'

'If the cap fits, wear it.'

Kev's eyes narrowed. 'I think you'd better take that back.'

Ant bridled. 'Make me.'

Kev stared at him for a moment then turned away. 'Let's just get on with the game, eh? What's the music today, Ratso?'

Ratso was about to answer when Ant took a step towards Kev.

'Think you can fob me off that easily, do you, Guv?' he asked. 'Well, I'm still waiting for an answer.'

Kev was keen to avert a fight, and continued to look away. That just made Ant even more angry.

'Don't walk away from me, McGovern. You're just like your mate. Too gutless to stay and face the music.'

'Is that Jamie you're talking about?' asked Kev.

'Got it in one.'

'Then I'll tell you something for free, Ant. Now I know what he's been going through, I reckon he must have more bottle than the rest of us put together.'

'You're talking rubbish.'

'Not half as much as you are.'

And that's when Ant snapped. He jumped on Kev and started laying into him with balled fists. Kev jabbed an elbow into Ant's face and rammed him against the lockers. It wasn't much of a fight. Ronnie came from nowhere and dragged them apart.

'I think you'd better cool off, Anthony,' he said. 'You're on the bench.'

Ant stared at the manager. 'You mean I'm dropped?'

'That's right. You can't take the field in that state.'

'And what about him?'

Ant was glaring at Kev.

'I think Kevin was provoked.'

'So you're dropping me, and leaving him on?'

'You're sub, Anthony,' said Ronnie patiently. 'If you calm down I'll bring you on later.'

But Ant didn't want to calm down. Shrugging off the restraining arms he stormed out of the changing-rooms. 'Well, you can stuff your rotten team. Hear that? I quit.'

Kev's shoulders dropped.

In five minutes they were going to take the field against the best team in the league, and not one Diamond player would have the heart for it.

The balance of the side was all wrong. For a start, they were light in defence. Mattie Hughes had come in to replace Ant, but he had none of Ant's composure on the ball. Every time Ajax pressed him, he stabbed the ball aimlessly away, conceding possession in front of his own goal. But that was nothing compared with the Diamonds' problems up front. Kev was partnering Dave. After Joey's poor performance in attack, it seemed the obvious thing to do. Kev was a natural striker of the ball. Unfortunately, it meant that the Diamonds didn't have him tackling in mid-field, and that's where Ajax were rampant. Kev watched as the lads in red and white raided down the right-hand side. His team was always on the back foot, and Ajax were exploiting every space that opened up. There was the feeling that a breakthrough was just a matter of time. Maybe this was it. Gord had just brought their wing-back down with a stern challenge, and two Ajax players were standing over the ball ready to take the free kick. It was dangerous, just four yards outside the penalty area.

'Get ready to rush them,' Kev bawled from the centre circle.

But nobody was listening. The Diamonds hung back as if dazed by the numbers Ajax had thrown up into attack. Their skipper drove the ball in low and hard. After a desperate scramble across his goal-mouth Daz managed to beat it down on the edge of the six-yard box, but he couldn't hold it. As the ball spun off his gloves, one of the Ajax players swivelled and volleyed. It was in the net.

They were one–nil down. The goal was greeted by raucous laughter from behind the goal.

Costello and Brain Damage. Who else?

'What a sickener,' said Dave.

Kev didn't reply. His eyes were on his enemies.

'Not doing too well, are you, McGovern?' smirked Costello.

'Drop dead.'

The poison pair just laughed.

The Diamonds tried to direct the game from the re-start, but Ajax's mid-field dominance continued. John and Ratso were doing their best, but they were being run ragged.

'This is desperate,' said Kev as Ajax once again surged forward in numbers. 'I ought to help them out.'

'Forget it, Guv,' said Dave. 'You heard what Ronnie said. You're playing in attack. You've got to trust the lads at the back to do a good job.'

As if to make a mockery of Dave's words, Jimmy ran the ball needlessly out of play on the left.

'Oh, wonderful!' groaned Kev, still aware of Brain Damage and Costello's mocking laughter.

'Getting battered, eh, McGovern?'

'Get a life, Costello.'

Kev's tormentors chuckled. They were getting to him.

'Rattled, McGovern?' called Brain Damage.

Just before half-time the Diamonds finally managed to conjure up their first scoring opportunity. Gord headed the ball strongly out of defence and Mattie helped it on its way with his outstretched leg. Bashir collected it on the left touch-line and dribbled past two players before chipping it over the last line of defence. Dave came in like a train but the ball bounced up at a difficult height. To the Diamonds' disappointment and Dave's disgust he could only deflect it over the bar.

'Hard luck, Dave,' said Kev. 'That was a good effort.'

'Not good enough,' Dave answered.

As if to prove his point, play switched immediately to the opposite end of the pitch. The Ajax goalie had punted the goal-kick hard and long down the centre of the field. One awkward bounce and the ball had cleared the Diamond's back four.

The one Ajax player who was forward must have thought all his birthdays had come at once. He gathered the ball and bore down on Daz in the Diamonds' goal. Daz was out smartly to snuff out the danger and managed to block the side-footed shot with his leg.

'Great save,' said Kev, watching from the edge of the centre circle.

What happened next seemed to sum up the Diamonds' morning. Gord hared after the loose ball only to slip on the greasy turf. The Ajax winger took advantage of his fall and ran into space.

'Cover the near post,' yelled Kev.

The shout did no good. The dispossessed striker was

up on his feet after Daz's save and only had to nod in the inch-perfect cross.

Three–nil down.

Costello and Brain Damage were almost dancing a jig. 'Three–nil,' they chanted. 'Three–nil. THREE-NIL.'

With Ajax winning possession from the re-start, the Diamonds were relieved to hear the piercing shrill of the half-time whistle.

'OK lads, I have to hold my hands up,' said Ronnie as the team flopped miserably on to the grass. 'Kev was right. I should have gone with a lone striker and kept Kev in mid-field. We're creating nothing.'

'We're not stopping them creating anything either,' said Kev. 'The scoreline could have been even worse.'

'Without Ant or Jamie, we'll have to stick with the same line-up,' said Ronnie. 'We've got to go after goals.'

'But I thought we needed Guv back in mid-field,' said Ratso.

'We do,' said Ronnie, 'So I'm going to try Jimmy up front with Dave. Ratso, you take Dave's position.'

The switch stemmed some of the Ajax attacks early in the second half. Kev's fierce tackling denied them the space to set up their raids down the flanks. 'This is better,' said Ratso, ten minutes into the half.

Kev's generalship had given his mid-field partners renewed confidence. It also shut up Costello and Brain Damage.

'Better,' agreed Kev, 'but not good enough. We're still not giving our front men any service.'

Daz bowled the ball out to John, who flicked it forward. Kev picked it up midway inside the Ajax half and looked for options. He knocked it infield to Dave who laid it off sweetly to Bashir.

'More like it,' Kev told himself. 'This is what we need.'

Suddenly the Ajax defenders were backing off as Bashir came across the penalty area and smashed in a shot. Their goalie parried it but only managed to clear it as far as Dave. He struck it first time. It took a wicked deflection off a defender and glanced off the top of the crossbar and out of play.

'Come on, lads,' shouted Kev, clapping his hands. 'That was a real chance. We can still get back into this game.'

For ten minutes it was one-way traffic, with the Diamonds pressing Ajax back into the final third of the pitch. But their luck was out. Dave and Jimmy both hit the woodwork, but the Ajax lead remained a clear three goals.

'We're never going to pull this back,' moaned John.

'Oh, do shut up,' said Ratso.

Bashir was again working down the left flank. He offloaded the ball to Kev and ran on to take the return ball. Escaping his marker's clutches, he pushed it square to Dave.

'Mine!' screamed Kev, bursting into the penalty area.

Dave hardly needed a written invitation. With scarcely any back-lift he floated the ball into the far post. Kev met it with a powerful header. They'd cut the deficit to three–one. He glanced at Costello and Brain Damage. Suddenly, they didn't seem quite so happy.

'Anything to say now?' Ratso asked John.

John shook his head. Unfortunately, the Diamonds hadn't turned the corner yet.

Kev was jogging along the touch-line when he saw somebody coming. Jamie's dad.

'What's he doing here?' he murmured to himself. He found himself looking at Costello. Could he have something to do with this? His thoughts were interrupted by a roar from the other end of the field. To Kev's horror, Ajax had gone straight down the other end of the field and scored themselves. One of the Ajax forwards had slipped Mattie and stretched his side's lead to four–one with an easy tap-in. Brain Damage was capering round the field with Costello on his back.

'You idiots,' Kev raged at his team-mates. 'You've got to concentrate.' Tapping his finger to his temple by way of illustration, he reinforced the point. 'Let your minds wander and we get tanked.'

As play resumed he was all too aware that he could have done with listening to his own advice. The arrival of Jamie's dad had stopped him in his tracks. He was as much to blame as anyone for the goal. It proved to be the killer. The absence of Jamie and Ant was suddenly being felt more keenly than ever. Confidence was draining out of the Diamonds. Even then, there was worse to come. With five minutes to go, Ajax broke through again. Ratso and John had been trying to play one-touch football in their own half, and it had broken down. Kev was aleady humiliated by the four–one scoreline. Five would be like acid burning through his soul.

'Close them down,' he yelled, pursuing the boy in possession. But Gord was backing off. It was down to Kev. Throwing out a leg, he tried to curl his foot round and take the ball off the Ajax player's boot. Instead, he took his ankle. The blast of the ref's whistle told him he was in trouble.

'I went for the ball,' he protested. 'Honest.'

The ref was already reaching for a card. Kev threw his head back in despair. Yellow would put him on the edge of suspension. Red would put him out of the Cup semi-final. There was a knot in his stomach.

'Dangerous play,' said the ref, brandishing the yellow card.

Kev gave a sigh of relief. He'd got away with it. There was a price to pay, though. Ajax scored from the free kick. Five–one.

Brain Damage and Costello kept up their barracking of the Diamonds to the end, and it was a dejected Diamonds side that trooped off the pitch at the final whistle. Kev looked around for Jamie's dad, but he'd gone.

'And we've got to face that lot in the semi-final of the Cup!' said John. 'They'll annihilate us.'

For once nobody was in the mood to contradict him. Not even Kev.

Eleven

We barely talked after the game. We just got changed in silence. Even Ratso. I think Ronnie must have decided to leave well alone, because he stayed on the pitch chatting to the Ajax manager. I don't know how he can do that. I can hardly look my team-mates in the eye after a defeat, never mind talk to the opposition. Football isn't a game to me. It's war in boots. And we'd just been taken apart. To make matters worse I'd let my stupid temper get the better of me. Now I know how the dragon felt after his run-in with St George!

It had been a rotten Sunday morning. Losing was bad enough, but losing in front of Brain Damage and Costello! That was like having teeth pulled without anaesthetic. Then there was Jamie's dad. Surely he couldn't have thought Jamie would show up. His appearance had put me on edge, and I couldn't get this nagging thought out of my mind. Had somebody had a word with him? Did Costello have something to do with it? But why should he? Sure, Costello had teamed up with Brain Damage, but why would they be after Jamie? Then it clicked. I remembered the way Jamie had gone for them that time after training. Besides, they knew he was in trouble. They were like vultures round a dying animal. They'd been like second shadows for weeks now. What trick was Costello going to pull? I couldn't suss it – but I knew it would be mega when it happened. I wouldn't put anything past him. Back on the old estate he was the bane of my life. He worries me a lot more than Brain Damage. The worst you have to fear from Brain Damage is a knuckle sandwich. Costello's dangerous in a different way. He's a head-worker, the sort of kid who'll keep a vendetta going for weeks, months, years. I know he's got me in his sights. He always did have. And if he can use Jamie's troubles to get at me he will.

He followed me home from the match. He didn't do anything, just walked with Brain Damage about twenty yards behind me all the way. When I got to ours he called out to me. You're finished, *he said.*

I stiffened. You know what, at that moment I really thought he was right.

PART THREE

Going For It

One

Kev could hear the phone ringing as he opened the door. He was barely inside when he heard Mum calling. 'That you, Kev?'

'Yes, why?'

Kev's answer came out as a sullen grunt. Ant hadn't shown for training and now John had gone walkabout. The Diamonds were in trouble and he was in a nark.

'It's Jamie on the phone.'

Kev took the phone. 'Jay?'

'How did you do yesterday? I've been climbing the walls wanting to know.'

'It was bad.'

'How bad?'

'Five–one.'

There was a long silence.

'That's bad,' Jamie agreed finally. 'Any other news?'

'I had a row with Ant. I think he's thrown his hand in.'

Kev heard the slow sigh at the other end of the phone.

'And John was missing tonight.'

He left out the bit about his booking. He had to spare Jamie at least a bit of grief.

Another sigh, then: 'I'm sorry, Guv.'

'What are you sorry about? It's Ant who should be apologizing. Where are you, anyway?'

'I can't say. Mum's orders.'

'I don't mean the address,' Kev told him. He felt a bit insulted that Jamie couldn't trust him, but he understood the secrecy. 'Well, what are you doing with yourself?'

'Not much, I'm in a grotty bed-sitter with Mum. Have you seen Dad?'

'No.'

That's when Mum started gesturing. She'd obviously been listening. Kev tried to wave her away, but she went on mouthing something.

'Hang on, Jay,' Kev told him. 'My mum's trying to tell me something.'

He put his hand over the mouthpiece. 'What's up?' Heavy exasperation in his voice.

'It's him, Billy Moore. He came round just before you got in.'

Kev nodded, then explained to Jamie. 'Looks like your old man's still on the warpath. He was round here while I was out.'

'He didn't turn up at training, did he?'

Kev shook his head, which is pretty stupid when you're talking on the phone. 'No, but he was nosing round the match yesterday.'

There was a sharp intake of breath, then: 'If he comes back, just keep shtum. Don't tell him anything.'

'Jamie,' Kev said, 'what's to tell? I don't know where you are, remember. I wouldn't, anyway. Best mates don't.'

Kev glanced round at Mum. She took the hint and went into the living room. 'Are you coming back?' he asked.

'I don't know. It's up to Mum.'

Kev heard a voice in the background. Mrs Moore must have been hurrying him up.

'We need you, Jay,' Kev told him. 'If Ajax batter us again, we're finished. The lads will vote with their feet.'

Jamie was a long time answering. 'I don't know what to say, Guv. I'll have to go. I'll phone you when I can.'

Kev hung up. Jamie wasn't the only one who didn't know what to say.

Two

Monday began as badly as Sunday had ended. It was raining. Somehow the overcast day reflected Kev's mood.

'Oh no,' he groaned as the school gates came into view. 'I've been expecting this.'

Bashir looked questioningly at Kev.

'Over there. It's Jamie's old man again. That's the second time he's been hanging round in as many days.'

The boys looked through the thinning crowds at the school gates. Billy Moore was sitting in his car with the window wound down.

'Could I have a word, Kevin?'

Kev spotted Costello keeping an eye on him. The eternal shadow. He was definitely up to something.

'Hello, Mr Moore.'

A smile in return, but superficial. For show only. 'Have you seen Jamie?'

'No.'

It wasn't exactly a lie. After all, Kev thought, he hadn't actually *seen* him. That helped him say it without embarrassment.

'I'm worried about him,' said Mr Moore. 'It's his mum. She's been acting oddly.'

Kev met his eyes, then looked away. Mr Moore obviously knew Jamie confided in him.

'I'm worried about them *both*,' he continued, a touch

too earnestly. Kev wanted to tell him to take a hike, but he was a bit too scared of him. He had those eyes that burn into you. 'It's just a misunderstanding. I want them back.'

I bet you do, thought Kev.

'I mean, a family ought to stay together. Don't you think so, Kevin?'

'Depends what you call a family,' Kev answered.

Mr Moore's eyes flashed angrily, but he didn't say anything.

'Jamie didn't want to go. I'm sure you know that.'

Kev recognized the tactic. Mr Moore wanted to put a wedge between Jamie and his mum. But Kev wasn't having any.

'It's nothing to do with me, Mr Moore.'

'Oh, I think it is, son. If you have any idea where they are, you ought to tell me.'

'I told you,' Kev answered firmly. 'I haven't.'

'That's not what Anthony tells me,' said Mr Moore.

'Ant's wrong,' said Kev. 'Jamie didn't tell me where he was, even when ...' He bit his lip.

'Even when what?' demanded Mr Moore. 'So he has been in touch.'

Kev stepped away from the car. 'No, I told you.'

'A phone call, was it?'

Kev retreated towards the school gates. Mr Moore got out of the car and advanced on him.

'When did he phone?' he asked menacingly. 'What did he tell you?'

Kev hated himself for letting even this much slip. 'He never told me anything. Just said hello, that's all, and asked how we did on Sunday.'

'Sunday? Oh, the match.' Mr Moore considered Kev's reply for a second, then bent forward.

'You're not helping Jamie, you know.'

His hand was on Kev's sleeve. Kev felt the touch like a brand and flinched. 'Leave me alone.' He could feel Mr Moore's hand through the material. It was actually shaking.

'I'll leave you in peace, Kevin, just so long as you tell me what you know.'

Kev noticed that Cheryl was watching from a distance. She'd been passing with her mates, but the confrontation had stopped her in her tracks.

'I told you,' Kev said in a quavering voice. 'He didn't really say anything.'

'Do you really expect me to believe that?' asked Mr Moore. 'You being such big mates, and all.'

Cheryl had detached herself from her mates and was edging closer.

'Jamie's mum warned him off,' said Kev. He felt disloyal, putting it all on Mrs Moore but this wiry, balding man scared him. It was his eyes. So intense. Kev decided he had to throw Mr Moore a scrap, or he would never let go.

Mr Moore's face twisted into a cynical grin. 'Now that does sound genuine,' he said. 'She's trying to poison my boy against me.'

Kev was still backing off. 'I can't tell you anything else,' he said.

He glimpsed Costello still hanging round. He'd been joined by Brain Damage and Tez. All three were watching and listening, taking it all in. As if Jamie's dad wasn't aggravation enough.

'Maybe not,' said Mr Moore. 'But Jamie will phone you again. I know he will.'

Kev shrugged defensively.

'And if he does,' Mr Moore continued insistently, 'you're going to tell me everything. I'll be seeing you again, Kevin.'

It was Cheryl's cue to join Kev. 'What's going on?'

Kev watched as Jamie's dad returned to his car. 'Jamie's dad. I think he's losing it.'

Before Mr Moore got in, he stretched across his windscreen to take something from under the wipers. A note.

'My little birdy,' he murmured, running his eyes over it. He re-read it, frowned, then tucked it into his breast pocket.

'Did you kids see anybody put this here?' he asked.

Kev, Cheryl and Bashir exchanged glances.

'No,' said Kev. 'Why, what is it?'

But Mr Moore wasn't saying. Without another word, he drove off. As if to rub salt in the wounds, Kev heard a familiar voice. Costello.

'Oh, I wouldn't like to be in your shoes, McGovern.'

Kev glared at him then pushed past.

'Still,' said Costello, 'if you don't tell Mr Moore what he wants to know, I'm sure there'll be somebody who can help him, some little birdy.'

Brain Damage and Tez laughed appreciatively.

Kev was half-way home before Costello's words started to worry him.

It was Cheryl who set him off. 'So what's this little birdy?' she asked.

Kev shrugged and remembered the smirk on Costello's face. He knew him of old, and there was one thing about his threats. They were never just hot air.

Three

If Jamie had looked out of the window once that afternoon, he'd done it a thousand times. Where was

Mum? A few things to sort out, she'd said. Won't be long, she'd said. So where was she? She'd been gone nearly three hours. Jamie paced the floor of the tiny flat. He sat down on the greasy couch and leafed through the latest copy of *Shoot*, but his mind was racing. He couldn't settle to anything.

'Where is she?' His voice echoed strangely in the empty flat. Like it wasn't his. That was how life seemed since the split. Not his own any more. He didn't go to school, he didn't see his mates, he didn't even go out. It was like being a prisoner.

The slow ticking of the wall clock was the only sound in the flat. A slow-motion woodpecker boring into his brain.

'Where is she?'

He was climbing the walls. He'd turned the television on three times but it was just horse racing and cartoons. Old ones. At a loss for anything else to do he turned it on again. Some old biddy whining on about a flopsy bunny. Kids' stuff. He switched off in disgust.

'Oh, come on, Mum.'

He found himself back at the window, twitching at the yellowish net curtains. He was willing her to come. He was actually getting scared. What if she'd run into Dad? He felt a warm flush over his face and neck. It was panic. And shame. Shame that he hadn't been completely on her side. He knew what the old man was capable of. What if … ?

Mum's key scraping in the lock put an end to his dark imaginings.

'Where've you been?'

Mum had a carrier bag in each hand. 'I told you. The solicitor's, then a bit of shopping. They don't half keep you hanging about in those places.'

Jamie knew she didn't mean the shops. 'What do you need a solicitor for?'

'What do you think?'

Jamie turned away. Solicitor. That made it final. She really was going for a divorce.

'Does that mean we're moving off the estate?'

'Don't go jumping the gun,' said Mum. 'All I'm doing at the moment is finding out where I stand.'

'But we won't be going home, will we?'

Mum was kneeling in front of the tiny larder fridge. 'How am I supposed to fit anything in here?' she wondered aloud.

'Mu-um.'

'What? Oh, going home, you mean?'

Jamie rolled his eyes impatiently.

'Me and your dad will have to sit down and sort that out.'

Jamie's heart leapt. 'You're seeing him. When?'

'Nothing's arranged yet. He'll have to calm down first.'

'But you are going to talk to him?'

Mum finally succeeded in closing the fridge door. 'That's what I said, isn't it?'

Jamie nodded. 'What about school, and the Diamonds?'

'I'm sorry, son, but you're just going to have to be patient a little while longer.'

Jamie nearly exploded. There's patience and patience. Patience is waiting for the second half to start, or for a fish to take the bait. Whoever said anything about living in limbo in a doss house in Sheil Road? 'You can't keep me stuck in here forever. This is driving me mad.'

Mum looked taken aback. 'Jamie, I thought you understood.'

'I do, Mum, but you can't call this living.'

She took a step towards him. 'It won't last much longer. You've got to understand, though. There's no going back. Not yet. The way your dad is, I wouldn't feel safe going near the house, or letting you near your friends.'

'But he isn't a monster.'

Mum shook her head. 'You've seen him, Jamie. When he blows, that's exactly what he is.'

The images of his dad standing over her flashed through his mind. He lowered his head. 'I know. Sorry, Mum.'

There was a knock at the door. It was Phil. 'I heard raised voices. Something up?'

Mum glanced at Jamie. 'No, just a little heart to heart. Jamie's bored.'

Jamie couldn't hold back a wry smile. Bored? If she was trying to understand how he was feeling, she hadn't even come close.

'Bored, eh?' said Phil. He looked around until his eyes lighted on Jamie's football. 'How's about a kick-around. We can go over to Newsham Park.'

Mum looked concerned.

'Don't look so worried,' said Phil. 'Half an hour can't do any harm. Coming, Jay?'

Jamie smiled. 'Anything to get out of this dump.'

Jamie chested the ball down and tapped it back to Phil. It felt better just to be out in the open air.

'Mum says she's going to sit down and talk to Dad,' he said. He liked the sound of his own words. *Sit down, talk*; there was hope in words like that.

Phil side-footed the ball back. 'I suppose they'll have to sometime,' he said.

'Mum said it was a definite,' insisted Jamie. 'And I've a feeling it's going to be soon.'

'Don't go getting your hopes up, Jay. She hasn't actually arranged anything. I'm not so sure Dad wants to talk.'

Jamie stood on the ball. He was frowning. Why did Phil have to put a dampener on everything?

'Of course he wants to talk.'

'Sure of that, are you?'

'Meaning?'

'Meaning I can't remember the last time they talked. Properly, I mean.'

'You're being stupid,' said Jamie. 'They're always talking.'

'Yes, but he does it with his fists.'

It was something Jamie had noticed about his brother. Phil found it hard to even say the word *Dad*. As if mentioning his name would be somehow going soft on him.

'I know he's done terrible things,' Jamie admitted. 'But I'm sure they could ...' He let the sentence trail. 'Even now.'

'You're not trying to tell me you expect her to have him back?' gasped Phil. 'After what he's done? You're mad, Jamie.'

'But she is going to get in touch. She promised.'

'Only to get the ball rolling. You know, separation and all that.'

Jamie felt like he was sitting on horseback. *Two* horses, and they were going in opposite directions.

'Oh, come on, Jay. We don't have to go through this all over again, do we? I thought you'd got used to the idea. Mum and the old man are finished. For good.'

Jamie knew his brother was telling the truth. Of course he knew. But somewhere inside he couldn't let it go. There was still hope. However flimsy that was, Jamie couldn't give it up. He wasn't about to tell Phil, but in his heart of hearts he knew it wasn't over.

Not by a long chalk.

Four

Jamie phoned again. He sounded really brassed off. All this business with his parents is turning him inside out. Sometimes it's like talking to two different people. He starts off by telling you how horrible his dad has been. Then in the same breath he's hoping there's some way for them to get back together. I can't say it's that strange, though. I'm probably the same. Dad let me and Gareth down again this week. He makes me so mad. Funny thing is, I get angry with Mum, too. Like she should have hung on to him or something. Yes, I know I'm being stupid, but that's the way it is with feelings. Somebody ought to write a book about it. 'How to feel when you're a kid and your parents are doing each other in.' It'd sell a million.

I asked Jamie if he would be playing again soon. OK, so it was insensitive, but you can't blame me for trying. We've got a league game against Orrell Park Rangers this Sunday, then it's the big one. The Cup semi-final against Ajax. I had one bit of good news for him, too. No, it wasn't about Ant. Daz couldn't make him change his mind. He's still staying away. It's John. Turns out he didn't have a grievance. He was laid up with the flu, that's all. He ought to be back on Sunday.

There was another thing I thought about telling Jamie, only I don't really know what to make of it myself. It's Costello. Him and Brain Damage are up to something. Everywhere I turn I run into them. A couple of times I've even seen them hanging round Jamie's house. They seem really interested in Jamie's dad all of a sudden. I just wish I could figure out why. In the end I didn't say anything. Why worry Jamie when it's probably all in my mind? Jamie listened to my news, but I don't think it made him feel much better. He says this flat he's staying in is the pits. Damp and trashy. Nothing to do, either. He hates it. I felt really depressed by the time I put the phone down.

Jamie's life is going down the pan, and with it any chance of the Diamonds pulling themselves together.

Five

It was the church bells that woke him.

'My second Sunday in this pigsty,' Jamie snarled out loud. 'Seven days in limbo.'

He expected his mum to say something, to come out with the usual excuses. But when he sat up he discovered that he was alone. Pulling on his jeans and T-shirt, he padded out on to the landing in bare feet.

'Mum?'

'I'm on the phone, Jamie.'

He was about to go back into the flat when Mum's words caught his attention.

'He didn't cause any trouble, did he?'

Jamie didn't know who she was talking to, but there were no prizes for guessing who she was talking about.

'But it was only verbal abuse? Thank goodness. It could have been worse. So what did you tell him?'

The pay phone was on the floor below but in the hush of a Sunday morning, Jamie could hear Mum clearly.

'No, no, you said the right thing, Dad.'

So that was it, she was talking to Gran and Grandad.

'Oh, he wants to talk, does he?'

Jamie leant over the bannister. That's right, Mum, he wants to talk.

'Well, I don't.'

Jamie's hands gripped the rail. But she promised.

'The only way I'm going to meet him is with a solicitor present. Oh yes, if he comes back you tell him that.'

Jamie took a step backwards. He was confused. Hadn't she told them there was going to be a meeting? To sort things. And now there was no meeting, and nothing sorted. He was going to be stuck in this stupid flat forever. No Dad, no mates, no school, no Diamonds, nothing. He felt sick.

The phone conversation continued. 'That's really good of you, Dad, but I've got my building society book. I can manage for a few more weeks. I'm seeing the solicitor again on Thursday. We might get some movement then. Yes, see you. Give Mum my love. Bye, Dad, bye.'

It was when he heard her footsteps on the stairs, that Jamie made his decision. He'd had enough. A whole week stuck on his own. Just because Mum said so. Well, he wasn't going to listen to her any more. She'd lied to him. She'd said she was going to sort things out and she hadn't. He reached for his trainers and pulled them on. If she couldn't keep her word, why should he? It's not like he was going to go running to his dad or anything. He wouldn't do that, not after the way he'd treated her. This wasn't about Mum, or Dad. It was about him, Jamie Moore. He just wanted to see his mates. He wanted to be alive.

Mum walked in. 'You're up, then.'

Obviously.

'I'd have let you talk on the phone. That was your grandad.'

'I know.'

'You mean you were listening?'

A surly nod.

'Your dad's been round causing trouble. They nearly had to call the police.'

'Call the police! On Dad?'

'He wouldn't go away. He started yelling and bawling in the middle of the street. He even told your grandad he was going to punch his lights out. And Billy knows he hasn't been very well.'

Jamie wasn't even listening. One idea had bored into his brain.

'They were going to set the police on Dad?'

'Jamie, they didn't want to. He was getting out of control. For a moment they thought he was going to put the windows in.'

Jamie stood up. 'That's what you say.'

'Jamie!'

He gave in to the overwhelming need to lash out. 'Well, it's not like you tell the truth, is it?'

Mum looked shocked. Just as she was supposed to. 'I don't understand.'

'You said you were going to talk. Then I hear you telling grandad you don't want to know. You lied to me, Mum.'

'I didn't, Jamie. I didn't lie.'

'Then what do you call that?'

'You're not listening. Of course I'm going to have to sit down and discuss things with Billy. But on my terms. When he's calmed down.'

The words had no effect. Jamie was sick of listening and he was sick of being knocked around by things he didn't understand. None of this was down to him. If

Mum and Dad had to fight then why not hurt each other? Why did they have to drag him in? He'd had it with them. Both of them.

'Jamie,' Mum said, taking his hands. 'You've got to understand.'

He snatched his hands back. 'I do understand. You lied to me. You're a liar.'

Then he was running. To the door. On to the landing. Mum calling behind him. Down the stairs. Mum running after him. To the front door and into the street. Mum's footsteps falling behind. To the street corner and across the road. Accelerating. Drowning out Mum's cries with the pounding of his heart and the beating of his shoes on the pavement.

Over the pelican crossing and on towards Breck Road. And Mum's voice in the distance. Dying away. Getting lost in the traffic.

Then he was alone.

Confused and alone, but most of all, free.

Six

There was a knock at the door. I ran to open it. Dad had promised to watch us against Orrell Park. As usual. But it wasn't him. As usual. It was my cousin Cheryl, offering a bit of moral support. That's not what I wanted at all, though. I wanted Jamie back and an end to his civil war with Ant. What I got was a shock to the system. It was something Cheryl said.

'Heard the latest?' she said. 'A little birdy told me that Phil's been seeing Jamie at school.'

I didn't answer. A funny little tremor went through me. It's like she'd come out with a magic code or something.

Little birdy. I'd heard it before. I had a feeling I'd been with Cheryl at the time. Pictures flashed through my brain. Jamie. And Costello. But that's all that came. Pictures. Not an explanation.

Brushing my thoughts aside, I stepped back to let Cheryl in. As she shoved past I saw Costello and Brain Damage. The nastiest double act since Bubonic and Plague. They were hanging round across the road. Tez and Jelly Wobble were also in attendance. There was nothing surprising about seeing them there. They only lived down the road. I frowned all the same thinking of the little birdy and the way they were always lurking round Jamie's house. We exchanged a bit of verbal, then I closed the door. Shutting them out of my mind wasn't so easy.

Seven

Jamie got to the Diamond early. There was still over an hour to go until the match. He thought of calling on Guv, but that would take him too close to home. He was angry with Mum, but not angry enough to expose her to Dad's rage. There was no way he was going to invite the old man to follow him. Turning up the collar of his jacket against the biting easterly wind, Jamie trudged along South Parade kicking an empty Coke can before him.

He was too preoccupied to notice Costello and his entourage coming from the direction of Owen Avenue.

'At least I'm out of that stinking flat,' he told himself. He needed the reassurance. He was starting to think he'd made a mistake. The only newsagent on the estate was there on South Parade. Dad could appear at any moment to pick up his *Sunday Mirror*. Jamie scanned the Parade for signs of him. He saw a young couple coming his way. The woman was pushing an empty buggy. The man was hoisting an excited toddler on to his shoulders. Jamie didn't see anyone else.

Not even Brain Damage hiding behind a parked Ford Transit van. Or Costello hiding behind Brain Damage.

Shuddering at the thought of bringing Dad's anger down on Mum, Jamie hurried to the end of the Parade, by the garages. He passed within a few feet of Costello and co. He missed the close scrutiny of their eyes. He missed Costello's whispered comments. He even missed Tez's departure with a crumpled note in his hand.

Kev and Bashir exchanged glances. Did Cheryl have to remind them of *every* defeat they'd suffered?

Kev was annoyed. 'You could give John O'Hara lessons, you know that?'

'In what, may I ask?'

'Miserableness,' Kev answered.

'Is that a real word?' asked Cheryl. She liked to tease Kev. Make out he was stupid. Which he definitely wasn't.

'You tell me,' Kev grunted. 'You're the swot.'

Cheryl wrinkled her nose. Behaving yourself and doing your best didn't make you a swot. Just sensible.

'I wonder what Brain Damage is up to,' Bashir said.

They were passing the garages. One of his favourite haunts.

'I'm more bothered about Costello,' said Kev. 'He's not like Brain Damage, he's got something between his ears. I hate him and the whole gang. They shouldn't be allowed near the pitch.'

'It's a free country,' said Cheryl.

'Well, it shouldn't be,' snapped Kev. 'Not for sewer rats like him.'

'Now aren't you in a lovely mood?' said Cheryl.

'Stow it,' said Kev.

And that's the way they were as they walked across the estate. Grumbling, squabbling, apprehensive. But quite unaware of Jamie killing time at the far end of the garages. Or Tez returning triumphant from his errand.

Billy Moore left home later than usual. Without Julie and Jamie the house seemed empty. He wasn't the sort of man who lay in bed late, but he did that morning. There was no reason to get up. He ran his electric shaver over his whiskers and scowled into the shaving mirror. The look was for his wife, but she wasn't there. With nobody to vent it on, his rage lay coiled in his stomach.

His frustration hung in the bathroom like a cloud. When he finally left the house to get a newspaper, he almost missed the note trapped under his windscreen wiper.

The fifth he'd had from his mystery informant. It was the appearance of his next door neighbour that alerted him to something flapping on his windscreen.

'Miserable weather, isn't it, Billy?' said the neighbour.

'Not half.'

Billy smiled and inspected the note.

If you want to see your Jamie, it read, *he's back on the estate*.

It was a child's handwriting. That didn't bother Billy. It was the news the note contained that mattered. He read on.

You'll find him down Jacob's Lane.
The note was signed: *A little birdy.*

Jamie heard voices from the other end of the garages, but he didn't recognize them. The wind muffled them, disguised them. He glanced at his watch. He'd killed nearly an hour. It would soon be kick-off. The voices seemed to be coming closer.

'Better to be safe than sorry,' he told himself. It could be anybody. Brain Damage for starters. Or that slimy creep Costello. He waited for the footsteps to die away. Convinced that they'd gone he slipped out and headed for Jacob's Lane.

He stayed alert all the way. He was determined not to do anything that might put Mum in danger.

Eight

It was a makeshift side that took the field against Orrell Park Rangers. Carl Bain had been pushed up to play in attack alongside Dave Lafferty, and Mattie Hughes was starting at the heart of the defence. Their presence didn't give anyone in the yellow and blue of the Diamonds much pleasure. Even Ratso's anthem on the ghetto-blaster failed to raise their spirits. The bust-up between Ant and Jamie hadn't only cost the Diamonds two of their star performers. It had punched a mile-wide hole through their confidence.

Right from the kick-off, Rangers were out to exploit their opponents' lack of shape. Their passing was accurate and full of confidence. Their tackling was sharp and well-timed. And their contempt for their ragged opposition was etched on their faces. Rangers were't just out to beat the Diamonds. They were going to bury them. Twice in the opening minutes Rangers came close to opening their account. Two shots from distance flashed across Daz's goal, sending him into a fine temper.

'You've got to get tighter on your man,' he fumed.

'Daz is right,' said Kev. 'You're getting done by their pace. You've got to get in quicker. Don't just huddle together waiting to be attacked, follow your man. Track him.'

But the Diamonds' defence didn't look like it could track a snail. When Rangers came again, nobody picked up on the run down the right. The winger mis-kicked it from the full-back's lay-off. But the Diamonds' problems weren't over. With Gord and Mattie at sixes and sevens, the ball ran loose to Rangers' unmarked striker. He made no mistake.

One–nil.

Kev shook his head. Their defending had been lame.

'I thought they'd turn up,' said Bashir, standing a few yards away.

'What's that?' Kev was still taking in the disaster on the field, 'Oh, wonderful. That's all I need.'

He watched Costello arriving, followed by Brain Damage, Tez, Jelly Wobble and two other boys.

'How are you doing?' chortled Jelly Wobble. Sarcasm was his middle name.

'You know exactly how we're doing, fat boy,' Kev shot back. 'Now do us all a favour, and lose yourselves.'

'No can do,' said Brain Damage coolly. 'We're here to see the action. *All* the action.'

There was something in the way he said it that sent a wave of anxiety through Kev. They weren't there just to needle the Diamonds. Something bigger was going down. But what? He glanced at Costello. He hadn't said a word. He didn't need to. There was a knowing look in his eyes that made Kev feel even more uncomfortable.

Rangers were back on the attack from the re-start, hitting the foot of the post and dropping a header on to the roof of Daz's net. They were out to stretch their lead, and there seemed precious little in the Diamonds' armoury to stop them.

'John, Mattie, Gord,' Kev ordered. 'Tuck in tight. You've got to break up these attacks. I can't do it all on my own.'

Which is just what he had been doing. Without Kev's tireless running and tackling, Rangers might easily have been leading three– or four–nil. And that was without their bagful of missed chances. The signs were ominous.

'Now look who's here.' It was Bashir talking again. Kev turned.

'Jamie.'

Jamie had no kit with him, but Kev was glad to see him anyway. Maybe the Moores were finally sorting themselves out. Then Brain Damage and Costello started with the bird noises. The rest of the gang soon joined in.

'What's up with that lot?' asked John.

'Beats me,' said Kev. 'Maybe they've flipped ...'

Suddenly his face drained of blood. 'Little birdy! Of course, that's why they've been hanging round Jamie's house. It's a set-up.'

Taking advantage of a break in play to collect the ball from the neighbouring pitch, Kev approached the dead-ball line. 'You've got to get out of here, Jay. I've just figured it out. The little birdy – it's Costello. He's been sending your dad letters.'

'Little birdy?' Still the look of confusion on Jamie's face. Then realization. 'Oh no.'

'What's wrong?' asked Bashir.

Jamie stared at Costello with undisguised hatred. 'You saw me earlier, didn't you?' he demanded.

Costello wasn't fazed. He just returned the look, a smug grin on his face. Brain Damage moved closer, ready to rumble.

'You did, didn't you? I can see it in your face.'

Still the smug grin.

'So now he knows I'm here. That's it, isn't it?'

Costello stretched out his arms in a faked yawn of indifference.

Jamie clenched his fists, then turned to Kev. 'Guv, I've done something really stupid. I've got to go.'

Kev nodded. 'Get on your toes, Jay, before it's too late.'

Play had resumed, but Kev couldn't take his eyes off Jamie. He glanced anxiously up Jacob's Lane. No sign yet of the Moores' Cavalier.

'Guv,' shouted Daz Kemble, 'Are you in this game or not?'

Drawn by Jamie's flight, Kev hadn't noticed the long throw from Daz heading in his direction. He was too late to stop the ball running out of play. Rangers' throw-in. As he waited for the ball to come back into play, Kev glanced again across the playing field. Jamie had reached the broken fence at the far end. And still no sign of Billy Moore. They'd rescued the situation. But that's more than he could say for the match. The throw-in was a good one. Plenty of distance and dropping right into the danger area, a few yards outside the penalty area. The Rangers striker tried to chip Daz.

The Diamonds' goalie was alive to it, but he was always stretching. He couldn't collect it cleanly and it ran loose. Somebody stuck out a leg. It crashed into the roof of the net.

Two–nil.

The whistle went two minutes later.

'Not before time,' said John, his face as bleak as the weather.

Nine

Jamie's heart was thumping in his chest as he scrambled up the embankment to the disused railway line which spelt safety. The council had been working on it for months, turning it into a cycle path. It would take him half the way back to the flat, and no chance of Dad seeing him.

'How could I be so stupid?' he asked himself angrily. 'Somebody was bound to see me.' And that somebody just had to be Costello.

'I'm sorry, Mum.'

He was just relieved to have got away with it. Guv was a real mate. Jamie knew he'd never have put two and two together and realized what Costello had been up to. But Guv had. He had a nose for trouble. That's what made him what he was, the Guv'nor.

'Good old Guv.'

Jamie strained to follow the play on the pitch, but it was hard to be sure what was happening. There were so many matches going on simultaneously. It looked like a lot of human ants flitting back and forth across a green games-board.

'Go on, Diamonds,' he urged, even though he

couldn't tell whether they were attacking or defending or still getting the half-time pep talk. For all the scare of thinking Dad might be on his way, he was starting to feel good. He'd got out of the flat and seen his mates with no dire consequences.

He permitted himself a smile. Then: 'I'd better make a move.'

Jamie was about to jog away down the cycle path, when something caught his eye. Just to the left of the changing-rooms somebody was moving. He took in the navy blue jacket, the black trackie bottoms and the white trainers. Oh, not now. Not when I'd got it all sorted. It was Mum.

He was tempted to call out to her, but what was the point? She would never hear from that distance. He would have to go and warn her.

As he hurried down the embankment he mumbled a little prayer. 'Please don't let Dad come. Not yet.'

Shoving through the broken slats of the fence he ran back towards the game. As he closed the distance between himself and Mum the ants turned back into people. The meaningless dots grew faces. The lads were clustered around Ronnie, getting their half-time instructions. Mum was moving towards them.

'Mum!' yelled Jamie. 'Go back.'

She'd spotted him and was waving. Jamie recognized the expression on her face. Anger that he'd run away, but mostly relief that he was safe.

'Mum, we've got to get away.'

She smiled in return.

'No, you don't understand. It's Dad. He knows.'

They were still too far apart. Mum was pointing to her ears.

Jamie ran on. 'Dad. He knows.'

Still the look of bewilderment.

Jamie got closer still. 'Dad knows. He'll be here any minute.'

At last Mum registered the warning. She began looking around anxiously.

'This way,' cried Jamie. 'Quick.'

But it was too late. At that very moment a K-registered Cavalier was pulling up on Jacob's Lane. Jamie saw the balding man climb out of the driver's seat and slam the door. He heard the yelp of the car alarm.

'He's here.'

Ten

Remember what I said about the hero inside my dad. Well, he came good all right. I don't know what would have happened if he hadn't shown up when he did. I didn't realize what was happening to start with. I mean, I thought Jamie was long gone. One minute I was trying to make the point that we had to stop the kick-and-rush stuff and start building attacks from mid-field, the next all hell broke loose.

Ronnie had been saying something about our movement off the ball when he broke off and looked to his left. About the same time we heard the screaming. Then Jamie's voice. 'Help me. He's hurting my mum.'

I took in the situation at a glance. Billy Moore had hold of his wife by the wrist and was dragging her towards him. She was pulling desperately in the opposite direction. But he was too strong. He yanked a handful of her hair and twisted her head round. Then he was yelling right into her face.

'I'm never going to let you walk out on me. You hear? Never!'

Jamie was hitting his dad and screaming for him to stop, but I don't think Billy Moore even realized he was there. He was too far gone. Jamie had told me about the rage that took over when his dad blew, but I'd never seen it. Not even that time outside school when he'd made me feel really uneasy. Now I had.

Ronnie tried to intervene, but if he thought sweet reason was going to work, he was living in a dream world. He tried to step between them, but Jamie's dad was beside himself. He struck out, catching Ronnie across the face. I saw Ronnie's look of surprise, then the stream of blood from his nose. It was a horrible feeling, knowing that nothing could stop Billy Moore.

It didn't last, though. Dad saw to that.

I didn't even see him arrive. No, it was his voice I heard. 'Leave her alone.'

Billy Moore carried on regardless. And that's when Dad put a stop to it. He brought the side of his hand down on Mr Moore's arm. The one that was holding Jamie's mum. It was a piledriver of a blow, carrying all Dad's strength. In almost the same movement, he twisted the arm and forced it up Mr Moore's back. An instant later he had wrestled him to the ground and had his knee in his back.

It was all over.

Unfortunately, there was still an unwanted postscript. One that would put me out of the semi-final.

Eleven

Kev watched as the taxi pulled away. He hadn't wanted to carry on with the match, but Jamie insisted.

'I'll be OK,' he said, as he climbed in beside his mum. 'Just get us back into the game.'

'Now,' said Kev's dad, slowly easing his hold on Billy Moore. 'Are you going to behave yourself?'

Everybody's eyes were on them.

'It's OK,' Mr Moore replied. 'I've calmed down.'

Kev knew it was true. He registered the look in his eyes, the sunken slope of his shoulders. It was something any footballer would recognize, the body language of defeat.

'You're not going to try anything?' asked Kev's dad.

He couldn't if he'd wanted to. The taxi was long gone, whisking Jamie and his mum to safety.

Mr Moore rose to his feet. He didn't meet anyone's eyes. He didn't speak. He just turned and started the long walk towards his car.

'Never a dull moment with this team of yours, is there?' said Kev's dad.

Kev just smiled. 'I'm glad you turned up.'

'It was about time, wasn't it?' said his Dad ruefully. That was as close to an apology as you got from Tony McGovern.

'Does that mean we can start the second half?' asked the referee timidly. He looked like he wished he'd never heard of junior football.

'Yes,' said Ronnie. 'Excitement over.'

It took a few moments to get all the players back on the field. Everybody was still talking about the events of half-time.

'You all right to play on?' Ronnie asked Kev.

'Of course.'

Inside he wasn't so sure. The way Jamie's dad had exploded had turned Kev's legs to jelly.

'I just thought ... You know, you and Jamie being such big mates.'

Kev smiled. 'You heard what he said, Ron. He told me to get us back in the game.'

Ronnie still looked concerned. 'If you're sure.'

'I'm sure.'

He wasn't. But everything started to change as he moved towards the centre circle. With every step the shakiness was fading. He was feeling good. After all, it was Dad who'd saved the day.

But he'd reckoned without Costello.

'Well, well,' he chuckled. 'Wasn't that a turn-up for the book?'

Kev glared. He'd completely forgotten about the architect of all the trouble. 'I'll see you about this later, Costello.'

'Don't worry,' said Brain Damage. 'We'll be right here, waiting for you.'

Kev scowled. The double act again.

The second half was a scrappy affair to begin with. The half-time incident had knocked Rangers completely out of their stride without doing much for the Diamonds' game. It was ten minutes before anybody could put their stamp on the match. And then it was Kev.

'Dave,' he shouted as the Diamonds' striker made a run.

Rangers had Dave down as the danger man. He was followed by two defenders. Which was exactly what Kev had in mind. A neat back-heel to Ratso switched the play abruptly, catching Rangers unaware. Looking up, Ratso swung a long cross-field pass to Bashir. Completely unmarked, Kev burst into the penalty area.

'Bash.'

The first-time cross came in hard and low. Kev met it with the side of his boot. The deficit was cut to one goal. At two–one down they were back in the match.

—— 126 ——

Rangers were tiring and Bashir was opening up their defence at will. They had no answer to his jinking runs down the left flank.

But Brain Damage did. With ten minutes to go and the Diamonds still trailing, Jimmy put Bashir away. The little winger beat two defenders in a touch-line hugging run.

'Bash,' shouted Kev. 'Cross it. I'm clear.'

Bashir looked up and steadied himself. If he could get the ball over, Kev would get a free shot at goal. And that's when Brain Damage struck. Taking advantage of Bashir's position right on the line, he poked out his foot and brought him crashing to the ground. Costello led the appreciative laughter. Brain Damage's intervention proved so outrageous that half the Diamonds team were converging on him.

'Now you've gone too far, Ramage.'

'That was disgusting.'

'He can't do that, ref. He's only a spectator.'

The Diamonds were angry. Kev was incandescent. Especially when he heard what the ref had to say.

'Sorry, lads, I was unsighted. I didn't see any infringement. Are you sure he didn't just fall?'

'Fall?' cried Dave. 'Have you seen the state of his shin?'

Bashir's leg was gashed just above the ankle.

'You're not going to finish the match, son,' said Ronnie. 'I can't risk it.'

'But we've got no subs,' protested Jimmy. 'What are we supposed to do?'

'I'm afraid we're going to have to play on with ten men,' said Ronnie.

Only it wouldn't be ten. Within seconds they would be down to nine.

Costello chose that moment to twist the knife. It was

the same old story. Brain Damage had done the physical stuff. The rest was up to Costello. 'That's the trouble with his sort,' he crowed, sneering at Bashir. 'No bottle.'

The red veil came over Kev's eyes. He took the law into his own hands. Brushing off Dave's attempts to restrain him he bunched his fist and smashed it into Costello's cheek. Brain Damage squared up but Kev laid into him too. The ref had no alternative. He showed the red card.

'Brilliant,' groaned Dave. 'You just had to do it, didn't you?'

Kev saw the grin on Costello's face. Bruised cheek or not, he knew he'd got one over on the Guv'nor.

'Well,' said Kev's dad. 'I for one think you were justified. Young Andy went a bit too far.'

Kev scowled. Young Andy! He thought of his dad's friendship with Brain Damage's thug of a brother, and suddenly he wasn't such a hero any more.

'Don't be stupid, Dad. I blew it. And I mean *really* blew it.'

On the field the Diamonds were doing their best to make amends. Even with nine men they were holding their own. Their sense of injustice at Bashir's injury and Kev's dismissal had stiffened a few backbones. Ratso and John were performing heroics in mid-field while Joey, Jimmy and Gord were rock solid at the back. There was only one problem. Without Kev's passing and Bashir's runs down the flanks, there was nobody to link up with Dave.

'Two minutes,' shouted Ronnie from the touch-line.

Daz had just gathered the ball at the edge of his area. He took the shout as an invitation to go forward himself. Giving the thumbs up, he set off downfield. It was his party-piece, had been since he joined the Diamonds.

He fancied himself as a bit of a Peter Schmeichel, an attacking goalie.

'I thought I'd told him to stop that,' groaned Ronnie. 'Get back between the posts,' he pleaded. 'What if the move breaks down?'

Daz pretended not to hear. There was no point going for the steady build-up. It was desperation time. As a concession to Ronnie's panic-stricken appeals, he launched the ball forward instead of running with it. He found his target. Dave took the ball on his chest and brought it down neatly. But he was facing his own goal.

'Hold it up,' Ronnie was shouting. 'And Daz, get back.'

Daz jogged back reluctantly and turned to watch the play. Dave was still shielding the ball from the two Rangers defenders who had closed him down.

'That's it, Dave,' hissed Kev, encouraging him. 'Give the lads time to get forward.'

Dave wasn't going to let the side down. Despite a couple of sly kicks on his calves he kept the ball, before flicking it sideways to the advancing Ratso. Having released it, Dave turned tightly, losing his markers. Suddenly he was advancing on goal. The full-back on the far side was keeping him onside. An accurate pass from Ratso and he would only have the goalie to beat. Ratso didn't let him down. It was slide-rule perfect.

'Yes,' cried Kev, knowing it was the Diamonds' last opportunity to get back on terms.

Dave took the ball in his stride and powered forward. His run drew out the Rangers keeper. Dave could sense a Rangers defender at his back. There was no time to tee it up. He had to hit it on the run.

'Goal!'

The Rangers keeper was pounding the turf. It had gone right under his body.

'Brilliant,' said Kev, applauding his side off the field. 'That's the sort of grit that could see us through next week.'

'What, with nine men?' said John. 'I don't think so somehow. Not against Ajax.'

'I could help,' said Daz. 'If you'd let me do my party-piece.'

'Over my dead body,' snapped Ronnie. 'You're staying firmly between those posts.'

'Listen, lads,' said Kev, 'I've got to own up. I know I let you down today, but we can still do it.'

Everybody stared.

'We can,' Kev insisted. 'I know we can.'

The question was: how?

Twelve

I'm still trying to handle the fall-out from Sunday's game. Oh, as far as I'm concerned it's a complete disaster. Ronnie phoned to confirm I'm suspended for the Cup semi-final. Me and my stupid temper! There's been one good development, though. Jamie turned up for school on Tuesday. Something to do with his Aunty Irene. It seems Ant's mum decided enough was enough. She had to get a grip of the situation. They had this big pow-wow. I had visions of a UN Peace Conference. I wanted all the gory details, but Jamie was a bit off-hand. I couldn't tell whether he was keeping his cards close to his chest, or whether he was genuinely in the dark. One thing was obvious. His dad was somehow under control.

I asked Mum about it when I got home from school. She was non-committal at first, then she started suggesting things. Maybe people were seeing the real Billy Moore for the first time. Maybe they'd started to understand what Jamie's mum had been going through. Maybe she'd gone to the police about him. It was all maybes, but it spelt out one thing. Something was getting sorted. Jamie wouldn't have to leave the Diamond for good.

There was another little item I was dying to ask Jamie about, of course, but I managed to bite my tongue. In the end, he came out with it himself. He was back and yes, that did mean he'd be playing on Sunday. Any other time it would have been great news, but I couldn't so much as manage a smile. Even Jamie's return wouldn't make up for me and Ant both being missing. The Diamonds were still on a hiding to nothing.

Thirteen

The fall of a hand on his shoulder made Jamie jump.

'Ant!'

Jamie, Kev and Bashir had been the first to arrive that Sunday morning, so there was nobody else in the changing-rooms to witness Ant's arrival.

Kev glanced at the holdall Ant was carrying. 'Does this mean ...?'

Ant nodded. 'If Ronnie'll have me back.'

Kev grinned. 'He'll snatch your hand off.'

Ant turned to Jamie. 'Truce?'

Jamie smiled. 'Sure, why not, but what's changed your mind?'

Ant gnawed at a scrap of loose skin on his thumb. 'It

looks like we were wrong … You know, about Uncle Billy and Aunty Julie.'

Jamie finished tying his bootlaces and sat up. 'Is that what your mum told you?'

Ant grimaced. 'It's what Uncle Billy told me. He's been acting really weird since last Sunday. You know, down in the mouth. Mum says the doctor's put him on tablets to control his temper.'

Kev laughed. 'I could do with some of them.'

Ant and Jamie gave him a dirty look and he fell silent.

'Anyway,' said Ant. 'Mum and Uncle Billy had a long talk last night. Mum's going to phone Aunty Julie later.'

Jamie glanced at Kev and Bashir.

'We can take a hint,' said Kev. 'We'll wait outside.'

Jamie watched them leave. 'Well?'

'Don't let on I told you,' said Ant. 'I'm not supposed to know about this.'

'My mouth's more secure than a combination safe,' said Jamie. 'Now give.'

'I overheard them talking. You and Aunty Julie can move back home. Uncle Billy's going to move into our spare room.'

'Seriously?'

Ant nodded. 'I think he's going to get a flat or something eventually.'

In his mind's eye Jamie saw the bed-sit and suddenly felt sorry for his dad.

'And Dad's happy with this?'

Ant rolled his eyes. 'I didn't say he was happy. But if Mum says it's going to happen, it'll happen.'

Jamie stared at the floor for a few moments. 'So that's that.'

It wasn't quite a happy ending, but it would have to do.

Ant nodded. 'Looks like it.' His voice fell to a whisper. 'Jay ...'

'Yes, what's up?'

'Sorry about the things I said.'

'Forget it, Ant.'

Ant looked over at the door where Kev and Bashir were barring the way to the rest of the Diamonds as they arrived. 'Think we should let them back in?'

Jamie stood up. It was his way of looking decisive. 'Why not? We're not going to beat Ajax without them.'

'Which brings me to our mid-field and forward play,' said Ronnie, getting to the meat of the team-talk.

John O'Hara gave Kev a meaningful stare.

'Yes, John,' said Ronnie. 'We're all well aware of Kevin's absence, and that's my main point of concern.'

Kev lowered his eyes. To say he was feeling guilty was an understatement.

'I'm making our Jimmy captain for the day. He's got a level head on his shoulders and he's involved in most areas.'

There was no dissension.

'Now, tactics. With Ant back in defence I'm happy to play a flat back four. We've got the defensive unit we're used to and I don't intend to tinker with it.'

'But what about me?' asked Mattie. 'Where do I play?'

'Who cares?' said Gord, just loud enough for everyone to hear. There was no love lost between them.

'Mattie,' Ronnie began, silencing Gord with an icy glare, 'you're going to be pushed up into mid-field. You, John and Peter ...'

There were giggles all round. Ronnie never used nicknames if he could help it, but Peter Ratcliffe was only recognizable as Ratso.

'You, John and Peter,' Ronnie continued, fighting for attention over the laughter, 'are going to be the ball winners. You can't afford to give this outfit any space. If you do—'

'Five–one,' said Kev, the scoreline of their last encounter saying it all.

Ronnie rubbed his chin thoughtfully. 'Exactly.'

'You're not giving us many options up front,' said Dave.

Ronnie glanced at Kev. He hadn't forgiven him the reckless attack on Brain Damage that had cost the Diamonds their key play-maker. 'I'm afraid we haven't got many. We've a couple of possible avenues, though.'

Now he had everybody's attention.

'First, there's our wing play. Jimmy and Joey are going to have to do a lot of work from the back, but you've got the legs. Then there's you, Bashir.'

Bashir returned Ronnie's look.

'You're the one who can give Dave the service he needs, but Ajax know all about you and I reckon they'll double up on the marking. So don't run yourself into the ground. Wait until they're stretched, then go for it.'

'You said there were a couple of avenues, Uncle Ron,' said Jimmy.

'There are, but they depend on holding Ajax in mid-field.'

John, Mattie and Ratso sat up on their bench.

'If we can compete with them there, we might be able to create something through the middle. Now, before I go on, have you got any questions?'

'Ron,' said Daz.

'Yes?'

'Can I go forward for corners? Only near the end, of course.'

Ronnie scowled. 'Any *sensible* questions?'

'I've got one,' said Kev.

'What's that?' sniped John. 'Who do we kick first?'

'Ha hardy ha,' said Kev, his neck reddening with embarrassment. 'No, what I want to know is why Ronnie spent half an hour talking to the Ajax manager.'

Ronnie smiled. 'I was coming to that. As you've probably guessed, I was fishing for information. Three names for you. First the mid-field pair that makes Ajax tick. Their skipper, Scott Geraghty.'

'He's the big, blond lad,' said Ratso.

'Right. His mate's called Kenny Mason. I tell you, they're a real handful. They seem to work by telepathy. Let them get on top of you and you've had it.'

'I know the other one you're talking about,' said Daz. 'Their striker, Craig Lennox. He goes to our school.'

'He's good all right,' said Ant. 'Dead strong.'

'That's it then boys. Close them down in mid-field, keep things tight at the back and try to break down the wings. Maybe later on they'll tire and we can work something down the middle. But that all depends on shutting them out for as long as we can.'

'Sounds simple,' said Mattie.

'You do, you mean,' said Gord. 'Don't forget they've already done the double over us.'

'Oh, and one other thing,' said Ronnie impatiently. 'For goodness' sake, work for each other.'

Ronnie reckoned the experience of sitting out the game on the touch-line would do Kev some good.

Oh yeah, Kev thought, like Christmas does turkeys good!

He sat next to Ronnie and Carl Bain with his jacket top zipped up half-way over his face. His way of trying to make himself invisible. Sitting twiddling his thumbs, he was starting to understand what a manager must feel like. Able to see what needs to be done, but stuck on the touch-line like a spare part. There was a decent crowd for the game, maybe fifty or sixty. Kev craned his neck to see if Dad had shown. No such luck. Two games on the run would be too much to hope for. Instead he glimpsed Costello. He had the whole gang in tow and he was holding court. Brain Damage was definitely playing second fiddle. Kev hated Costello. Nothing stopped him. He just bounced back.

'What, not playing today, McGovern?' he chirped sarcasticlaly as he caught Kev's eye.

Kev buried his face deeper in his jacket. If the Diamonds lost he was going to have Costello. The season would be over and he'd have nothing left to lose.

Still, it was the business on the pitch that mattered. Kev saw Ratso with his ghetto blaster. The Diamonds took the pitch to the strains of Johnny Tod, the Everton anthem. It would lift most of the team. Kev just hoped the Liverpudlians in the side wouldn't take exception to it. Jamie waved. He seemed to be getting on top of this thing with his parents. It was about time he got his mind back on the Diamonds, Kev thought. If he was going to return to form, today was the day to do it. Without making it too obvious, Kev crossed his fingers and wished for a miracle. Against Ajax that's exactly what they were going to need.

Fifteen

The Diamonds had lost the toss and they were playing into the sun. After a heavy overnight downpour the sunlight was strong and garish.

'Terrible, isn't it?' said Ant. 'I'm finding it hard to pick anyone out.'

Jamie shielded his eyes. As if Ajax didn't have enough going for them. They stood silhouetted against the glaring sun. It made them even more menacing. Geraghty was on the ball and he was working down the right flank. It was a slow build-up, patient, teasing out the weaknesses in the Diamonds' defence. He rolled it to Kenny Mason then crossed the half-way line to receive it back.

'Don't be drawn forward,' shouted Ronnie. 'Just keep a good line.'

Geraghty looked up and spotted his full-back moving into space on the left. Dropping his shoulder he went past Mattie and confidently struck a cross-field ball. The deft pass changed the point of the Ajax attack.

'Joey,' shouted Gord, 'Go out to meet him.'

But the full-back had the beating of Joey Bannen and was able to get to the dead-ball line without a serious challenge.

Kev jumped to his feet. 'Block him!' he was yelling.

'That's a job you'd be doing,' observed Ronnie. 'If you hadn't lost your rag.'

The full-back got his foot round the ball and flighted it across the goal-mouth. Craig Lennox powered in but Daz was alive to the danger. He tipped it over the bar for a corner.

'You shouldn't have committed yourself, Joey,' said Daz.

'But Gord said—'

'Since when was Gord captain?'

'Cover the post, Joey,' ordered Jimmy, reminded that that was his job.

It was a poor corner and Daz had no trouble gathering it. As the Ajax players streamed back towards their own half, he put Jimmy away with a tremendous throw-out. Jimmy sped along the touch-line aware of Bashir making a diagonal run infield. Hanging on to the ball until Jamie and Dave could get into the box, he rolled it square to Bashir who flicked it on into the penalty area. Dave chested it down and Jamie swivelled and hit it on the volley.

One–nil.

'Looks like he's back,' said Kev.

Ajax were stunned. They were runaway leaders in the league and they'd already done the double over the Diamonds. They clearly hadn't expected the opposition to make much of a game of it.

'Excellent,' commented Ronnie. 'But keep your concentration. They'll be going for the jugular.'

Jamie was wondering who this juggler was when Ajax mounted their retaliation. Scott Geraghty and Craig Lennox both went close with shots from the edge of the penalty area, and only a couple of scrambled clearances by Ant kept them out.

'Mark him,' shouted Jimmy, jabbing a finger at Kenny Mason who was drifting ominously into space. '*Mark him!*'

Unfortunately it was Mattie who took the job. He was a willing tackler, but Mason had him for pace. Leaving Mattie for dead, Mason continued his run into the area. Jimmy was the next player to try to tackle him, but Mason was strong and balanced and shrugged off the challenge. Just when Daz had decided the Ajax mid-fielder was going to take it all the way and started to come off his line, Mason slid a cushioned pass across the goal-mouth. Craig Lennox was in the perfect position to sidefoot it home. Ajax were back on terms.

One–all.

'Sucker goal,' grumbled Kev as he heard Costello and Brain Damage leading the mocking laughter a few yards away. 'What sort of tackle was that? This *is* a contact sport.'

Ajax didn't need advice to that effect. They were at the top end of the age qualification for the league, due to move up at the end of the season into the under-fourteens. Twelve months older than the Diamonds, they were correspondingly stronger, and it was beginning to show.

'My flaming ribs,' croaked Ratso after a jarring challenge. 'These lads are playing for keeps.'

It was the same story in every individual duel across the park. The Diamonds were contesting the game hard, but they were starting to come off second best. Much to the delight of Costello and company.

'Ajax have won control of mid-field,' Kev murmured to Ronnie.

'I know, Kevin.' Ronnie consulted his watch. 'Ten minutes to half-time. If we can just stay level until the interval.' He strode down the touch-line. 'Come on, lads,' he shouted. 'Keep it tight.'

The Diamonds did their best, but Geraghty was running the show, winning the ball and spraying out telling passes at will. No sooner had the Diamonds cleared their lines than he was putting them back under pressure.

'John, Ratso,' cried Kev urgently. 'Double up on him.'

'What's this?' asked Ronnie. 'You appointed yourself manager, have you?'

'Sorry, Ron.'

Ronnie gave him a level stare then shouted. 'Get on Geraghty. Double up if you have to.'

Kev gave a wry smile.

But Ajax wiped it off with a minute of the half remaining. Ant was racing back facing his own goal to roll the ball back to Daz, when Kenny Mason came from behind to put him under pressure. Kev saw the deliberate push that sent Ant sprawling. So did Ronnie and Carl who were on their feet pointing. Everybody saw the infringement.

Everybody except the ref. As the Diamonds appealed for a free kick he waved play on.

'Oh, come on!' protested Ronnie.

Kev was surprised. Ronnie rarely contested a ref's decision.

Daz did his best to salvage the situation, charging out gamely to block Kenny, but the Ajax player was on fire. Pushing the ball to Daz's left he stretched and struck it into the far corner.

Another huge roar from Costello's gang.

'Two–one down,' groaned Kev. 'And right on half-time. What a killer.'

Ronnie nodded. They both knew the goal would have knocked the stuffing out of the Diamonds. They would take some lifting.

Ronnie gave it his best shot. He praised the players to the hilt, talked them up as if it was them who were in the lead, then gently made the point that they had to do something about Geraghty. John wasn't having any, though. He was his usual helpful self.

'We're lucky it isn't more,' he moaned. Then he started sniping at Mattie, blaming him for Ajax's success in mid-field. He even started comparing Mattie to Kev. 'Guv would have done something about it.'

Kev wasn't flattered. He was annoyed. 'Oh yeah. Like when they turned us over five–one!'

All eyes were on Kev. The Diamonds were desperate for some inspiration.

'You want to know what I think,' Kev started.

They obviously did.

'You really want my opinion?' His mind was a complete blank. 'Well,' he began, trawling his brain for even the ghost of an idea. He was under the spotlight and it was making him sweat. 'I'll tell you what I think.' A long pause, then he had it. 'We put Jamie on Geraghty. Man-mark him. Neutralize the dweeb.'

'And who up front?' asked Dave.

'You.'

'But we've got to go after the equalizer,' said Jimmy.

'Says who?' Kev was warming to his theme. His crazy idea had got a life of its own. 'I'll tell you what Ajax have got. Patience. They're not chasing after goals. They build slowly out of mid-field.'

'True,' said Ratso. 'But they've got Geraghty.'

'And we've got Jamie. He got the goal, remember. Cool as ice the way he did that.'

Jamie looked horrified. Like he didn't want the burden of responsibility.

'We battle in mid-field,' Kev continued. 'And if we keep at it the breaks will come.'

Jimmy looked at his Uncle Ronnie. 'Well?'

Ronnie smiled. 'I'm with Guv.'

The lads did a double-take. Since when did Ronnie

use the boys' nick-names. Since Kev had bailed him out of trouble, that's when.

Kev watched the Diamonds take the pitch.

'Think it'll work?' Ronnie whispered.

'Doubt it,' Kev hissed back.

They both laughed.

Sixteen

Ajax realized they were in a game the moment Geraghty got his first touch. Jamie was determined to work to his brief – in like a shot, taking man and ball. Kenny Mason was none too happy at the way Jamie bundled his team-mate to the ground, and he showed it.

'See that, ref. Tackle from behind.'

Kenny was squaring up to Jamie, while Geraghty rolled on the ground.

'He'll be short-listed for an Oscar,' Kev announced loudly.

'Calm down, lads,' advised the ref.

'Calm down?' cried Kenny. 'What about the tackle from behind?'

'Looked like he got the ball to me,' said the ref, and awarded the Diamonds a throw-in.

Still Kenny argued the toss. 'The other way, surely.'

'It bounced off your man,' said the ref. 'And no more disputing my decisions or you'll be cautioned.'

Kenny was gobsmacked. 'But—'

Geraghty was hobbling theatrically to his feet. 'Leave it, Ken.'

Bashir collected the throw and tried to make ground down the left, but Ajax were alive to his runs and closed him down. They started to work it back down the middle of the park. Inevitably it went to Geraghty.

'He's recovered quickly,' noted Kev.

Once more Jamie did his job, sliding Geraghty. For a moment it looked as if he'd dived in too early. He went to ground and Geraghty hurdled his legs. He looked to be clear. But there was more to the Diamonds' midfield than Jamie, and Ratso was on hand to tidy up. Geraghty stood with his hands on his hips, as if tackling him wasn't in the rule book. He wasn't used to being hurried.

'What are you doing, Scott?' demanded Kenny Mason. 'You're not supposed to let a little wimp like that get one over on you.'

It was music to the Diamonds' ears. Ajax were quarrelling among themselves.

'It's working,' said Ronnie. 'They're used to teams being in awe of them.'

Kev nodded. 'We still need goals.'

'I thought you said they'd come,' said Carl Bain, the sub.

Kev exchanged glances with Ronnie. They would, wouldn't they?

By midway through the second half the middle third of the field was a battle ground. Geraghty and Mason were booked for Ajax. John and Jamie picked up yellow cards for the Diamonds. But nobody was easing up. For Aintree a possible league and cup double was at stake. For the Diamonds the Challenge Cup was all they had left and they weren't about to roll over and die. Even Bashir started to get in on the act. He'd lost the ball to his marker but tracked him back and cheekily dispossessed him on the half-way line.

'Did you see that?' asked Ronnie, stupefied. 'I didn't think that was part of his game.'

'I saw it,' said Kev. 'But I don't believe it.'

Oblivious to the comments from the touch-line, Bashir looked up. Dave was making a forward run and Jamie was breaking out of mid-field. The Diamonds' winger punted the ball upfield.

'Mine!' roared Jamie. Dave peeled away to give him a passing outlet.

Jamie was about to thread the ball through when he was chopped down from behind.

'That's an automatic booking,' said Ronnie.

'It's a sending-off,' said Kev, correcting him. 'That's Geraghty and he's already got a yellow card.'

The ref called Geraghty over. Judging by the look on the Ajax skipper's face he wasn't the only one who thought he was going to get his marching orders. But the ref confined himself to a stern lecture.

'Oh, well done, ref!' snorted Kev sarcastically.

Jamie tested his ankle gingerly.

'You all right?' asked Dave.

'Roll the ball in my path and I'll show you,' whispered Jamie with a sly wink. Ajax didn't have a monopoly on play-acting.

Dave obliged and Jamie pulled the trigger. The shot took a wicked deflection from the Ajax centre-back.

Two–all.

Kev gave Costello a meaningful glance. Not laughing now, are you?

'You never whistled, ref,' protested Geraghty. 'We weren't ready.'

The ref gave a slight smile. He knew Geraghty had got off lightly with a verbal warning.

'The ref owed us that one,' said Kev.

Ronnie winked his agreement.

Suddenly it was all Ajax again. Stung by the equalizer, they were flying. They were peppering the

Diamonds' goal with shots and headers. Only a string of athletic saves by Daz kept them out.

'The lads are tiring badly,' said Kev. 'Just look at Mattie.'

The player in question was bent double, trying to catch his breath.

'Fancy joining the fray, Carl?' asked Ronnie.

Carl nodded.

'The substitution will give us a breather,' said Ronnie, catching the ref's eye. He brought Mattie off.

Carl was no great shakes. He had the technique of a geriatric lobster, but he was fresh and helped stem the tide of attacks.

'It's going to extra time,' said Ronnie, looking at his watch.

'It can't,' said Kev. 'We've nothing left. Just look at everyone. They're shattered. Ajax are even lining up a couple of subs. Fresh legs. We'll get ripped apart.'

Ronnie threw up his arms. 'Carl was our last squad player. I'm all out of ideas. What do you suggest?'

Kev indicated their giant keeper. 'There's always our secret weapon.' He meant Daz's party-piece.

Kev looked at Ronnie. 'Well?'

Ronnie rubbed his chin. Ajax had just hit the cross-bar. 'We're dead on our feet, aren't we?'

Kev nodded.

'I must be mad.'

'You mean we're giving it a go?'

'OK, let him off the leash.'

Kev ran the length of the touch-line, past Costello, Brain Damage and their mates.

'Daz, Daz,' he yelled. 'Do it!'

He saw the broad grin. This had to work.

Craig Lennox was bearing down on Daz's goal. Seeing Daz coming out he tried to chip him. Which is when Daz did it. Instead of handling it, he headed it down and started dribbling forward. For a few momenta Ajax were too surprised to even attempt a tackle.

'Get back in your goal,' yelled Jimmy frantically.

'Can't,' shouted Daz, 'manager's orders.' And he surged forward.

As he continued his run, John put his hands to his head. 'He's flipped.'

Ratso agreed. 'I don't believe this!'

Kenny Mason finally attempted a tackle and quickly wished he hadn't. He just bounced off Daz's chest.

'Daz!'

Suddenly everybody saw the possibilities. They were all moving forward and shouting for the pass. A law unto himself, Daz ignored them and closed on the penalty area.

'Daz!'

Just when it looked like he was going all the way on his own, Daz surprised everyone. He stopped and pushed it square to Jamie. Jamie's mind flooded with a bitter memory. He remembered the sour taste of being dropped and the feeling of letting everybody down. Pausing only to get the goal in his sights he hit it. No subtlety. He wanted to break the net.

'Goal!'

Jamie immediately found himself buried under an avalanche of bodies.

'We did it,' Ratso was shouting excitedly. 'We did it!'

'You've done nothing yet,' warned Kev.

'Guv's right,' shouted Ronnie. 'Cut the celebrations and concentrate.'

It was easier said than done. The game was moving into stoppage time and the Diamonds had relaxed. Surely it was all over.

Scott Geraghty disagreed. 'Get forward!' he bellowed.

Craig Lennox was already racing across the Diamonds' penalty area, arm raised.

'Pick him up somebody,' shrieked Kev. 'You can't throw it away now.'

Craig took the ball down and went to hit it on the half-volley. Suddenly realizing the danger, Gord threw out a foot. It hit Craig a glancing blow on the hip, but the Ajax striker's hands flew to his face. A second later he was rolling round the pitch in mock agony.

'What's he doing?' asked Ronnie.

'Getting them a penalty,' replied Kev. 'What do you think?'

As the ref whistled for the spot-kick, Ronnie turned his back. 'I can't look.'

Costello and Brain Damage were going wild. 'Thought you'd won, didn't you, Diamonds? Well, tough.'

Geraghty placed the ball on the spot.

Statistic-king Ratso knew his ominous record. 'Nine penalties so far this season. Scored every one.'

Daz stood toe-to-toe with Geraghty, trying to psych him out, then very deliberately walked backwards to his line. At least half the Diamonds turned away, especially Gord. With the help of Costello's taunting, they all knew they'd squandered a three–two win. Geraghty stood hands on hips, waiting for the whistle, then started his long run up. He was going to blast it. Daz watched impassively. To Kev, even his large frame seemed hopelessly inadequate. He was wrong. Geraghty achieved tremendous power with the kick but he'd hit it straight at the keeper. Instinctively, Daz raised his hands. The ball smashed into his gloves and flew into the air. Blasted off his feet by the power of the shot, Daz tumbled backwards. And that's where he stayed, his studs tangled in the net. The ball started dropping.

'Clear it!' cried Kev.

Jamie and Geraghty reacted at the same time, lashing at the spinning ball. Jamie got there fractionally before the Ajax player and hammered it out of play. As Kenny Mason scampered away to retrieve it, the ref blew. Full-time. The Diamonds were through to the Cup Final.

Eighteen

So that's it. We're through to the Cup Final. You should have seen the Ajax lads. Gutted. Some of them were in tears. I'd have been the same. Yes, even me. That's what football means. You hear people who don't like the game: 'Seems daft to me,' they say. 'Twenty-two idiots running about after a bag of wind.' Don't they understand anything? It's more than just a game. It's a battle, a war even. For the duration of the match it's a struggle between good and evil, hope and despair. Win and you're a hero, lose and you're lost too. Brain Damage doesn't really understand it, but he doesn't play. Costello understands. That's what makes him dangerous, especially now he's the leader of their sick little outfit. He knows exactly what it means to me. That's why he came along, to see me fall. I didn't though, did I? I got away with it. When we get to that Cup Final, I'll be the Guv'nor again. I'll be the ice man, the ultimate control freak. Martians could land and I'd stay focussed. Nothing's going to faze me. I intend to be part of a memorable victory.

By the way, I got one over on Costello after the match. I did it as Jamie came off with the ball. I was dead sly.

'Jay,' I whispered, 'Roll it to me.'

'Why?'

'Just do it, OK?'

Jamie obliged.

'Costello,' I called, teeing it up.

He turned and I hammered it right at him. Nearly took his head off. He had to go home with the muddy imprint of the ball over half his face. He deserved it. I just wish I could have got Brain Damage too, but you can't have everything. Besides, he was looking pretty cheesed off, so I wasn't that bothered.

Oh yes, I nearly forgot. Jamie went back home yesterday. Him and his mum. His Aunty Irene is keeping tabs on his dad, but Billy Moore looks done in to me. He's just going to have to live with the fact that his temper didn't destroy Mrs Moore. It destroyed him.

It's weird when I think about the Moores. I mean, there was a time I actually wanted to trade places with Jamie. I still find it hard to believe that the perfect family's split up. I mean, they seemed to have it all. They were the ultimate Normals. Just look at them now. I don't get it. Maybe nobody's normal, after all. Either that, or we all are.

The main thing is, Jamie's got his life back. Sure, it's not perfect, but he can live with it. He's got a mum and a dad – just! – and he doesn't have to watch them tearing each other apart and him with it. I'm amazed it took me so long to see it, but we're alike, me and Jamie. We spend half our lives caught in the crossfire between people we love, but we survive all the same. That's what makes us winners, I suppose.

And we are winners, every one of us. Ant's come through and made his peace with Jamie, Bashir's learning to face down the rats who want to make his life a misery, and

Costello and Brain Damage have had to crawl back down the sewer where they belong. Oh, I know, they'll be back once they've licked their wounds, but we'll be ready for them. We've come through. We had to.

After all, we are winners.

Other books you might enjoy in the TOTAL
FOOTBALL series

Some You Win ...

'There's me with my mind full of the beautiful game ...
and what are we really – a bunch of deadbeats ...'

But Kev has a reputation to live up to and when he
takes over as captain of the Rough Diamonds he pulls
the team up from the bottom of the league, and makes
them play to win ... every match.

Under Pressure

'The pressure is on. Like when you go for a fifty-fifty
ball. Somebody's going to blink, and it isn't me. Ever.

Kev, captain of the Rough Diamonds, acts swiftly
when too many of the lads just aren't playing the game
and let pressures off the pitch threaten the team's
future.